The Mistletoe Mystery

By Nita Prose

The Mistletoe Mystery

The Mystery Guest

The Maid

The Mistletoe Mystery

A Maid Novella

NITA PROSE

Ballantine Books
New York

The Mistletoe Mystery is a work of fiction. Names, characters, places, and incidents are the products of the author's imagination or are used fictitiously. Any resemblance to actual events, locales, or persons, living or dead, is entirely coincidental.

Published in the United States by Ballantine Books, an imprint of Random House, a division of Penguin Random House LLC, New York.

BALLANTINE BOOKS & colophon are registered trademarks of Penguin Random House LLC.

LIBRARY OF CONGRESS CATALOGING-IN-PUBLICATION DATA

Names: Prose, Nita, author.
Title: The mistletoe mystery: a maid novella / Nita Prose.
Description: First edition. | New York: Ballantine Books, 2024.
Identifiers: LCCN 2024026331 (print) | LCCN 2024026332 (ebook) |
ISBN 9780593875445 (Hardback) | ISBN 9780593875452 (ebook)
Subjects: LCGFT: Detective and mystery fiction. | Novellas.
Classification: LCC PR9199.4.P7768 M57 2024 (print) |
LCC PR9199.4.P7768 (ebook) | DDC 823.92—dc23/eng/20240617
LC record available at https://lccn.loc.gov/2024026331
LC ebook record available at https://lccn.loc.gov/2024026332

Printed in the United States of America on acid-free paper

randomhousebooks.com

1st Printing

First Edition

Book design by Virginia Norey
Title page art: amovitania/stock.adobe.com

To Tony,

For his love of the season and so much more

The Mistletoe Mystery

Chapter 1

My gran loved all holidays, but her favorite by far was Christmas. Every year, when December rolled around, she'd take out the Advent calendar she'd made herself, repurposed from an index cabinet discarded by a library after computers rendered the card catalogue system obsolete.

Gran polished that cabinet until the grain was tiger-striped and golden. On each one of the twenty-five tiny drawers, she hand-painted a date in December, and below each number, she added a Christmas-themed flourish—a snowflake for December 3, a Santa hat for December 12, and for Christmas Day, the three Magi, heads bowed, each wise man cradling a glorious gift in his palms.

When I was a child, and well beyond, Gran would fill each of those twenty-five drawers with a wondrous treasure she'd scavenged for all year long and had saved just for me—a soft-pink seashell, a cherry chocolate wrapped in red foil, a miniature silver spoon.

On December 1, she'd bring home a fresh-cut Christmas tree given to her by the Coldwells, the last family she'd worked for as a maid. We'd haul that tree up several flights of stairs, dragging it into our apartment and festooning it with popcorn garlands and an assortment of homemade ornaments.

Then, on Christmas Day, we'd wake up early, and still in pajamas, we'd open our presents. One year, Gran made me an entire crate of orange marmalade, my absolute favorite. Another year, she gave me a silver necklace, a gift, she said, given to her by a dear friend decades earlier. I gasped when I opened the box and saw the chain shimmering against the white cotton batting.

"But it's your necklace, Gran," I said. "I can't accept this."

"Of course you can. It will look lovely on you."

And so it did. I wore that silver necklace from that day forward.

But no sooner had I received the beautiful gift than I recognized a new problem. "Oh dear," I said.

"What's the trouble?" Gran asked.

"The gift I got for you is useless now," I replied.

I picked up the parcel I'd wrapped for Gran in brown paper and topped with a red satin bow. My gift to her was a heart-shaped jewelry box I'd thrifted from a nearby store. Pure brass, it was filthy and tarnished when I bought it, which is why I got it for next to nothing. I polished and buffed that heart until it gleamed and glowed.

"Oh, Molly," Gran said when she opened it. "It's a beautiful jewelry box."

"Beautiful but useless," I said. "You have nothing to put in it now." We both knew that the only jewelry Gran possessed was the necklace she'd just given to me.

"No matter. I shall treasure this gift always."

She placed that heart-shaped box on her bedside table, where it remains to this day.

Each year when the holiday season rolls around, I find myself taking stock of my life and ruminating about Christmases past. Gran died several years ago, and yet here I am, remembering her fondly at this special time of year. After Gran died, I thought I'd never know joy again, that I'd spend the rest of my existence living like a mushroom in the dark. But it is not so. I live with my beloved boyfriend, Juan Manuel, who reminds me how to shine. He's a beacon of light adding hope and good cheer to all of my days. Sometimes, I have to pinch myself. My life is so good, I wonder if it's actually real. And if it is real, will it last?

It's silly, I know. And I try not to let doubts like these take hold, but they do get the better of me at times. Still, the truth is that Juan and I have lived together harmoniously for these past few years, sharing our modest little apartment and happily working at the Regency Grand Hotel. Whenever the calendar changes over to December, as it did about three weeks ago, Juan's natural enthusiasm dials up even higher than usual. He infects everyone—including me—with his buoyant Christmas spirit. His joy is contagious even in the darkest of times. For this reason, and for countless others, I cherish him so much that I don't know what I'd do without him.

With every Christmas that passes, Juan adds a new tradition to our holiday—a tradition à la Juan, as he likes to say. His fanciful rituals are wholly concocted by him, expressions of charity, mirth, and above all else, joy.

The first Christmas we spent together, I told Juan about Gran's Advent calendar tradition, and since then, he's kept that custom alive.

"I declare this the Month of Molly yet again," he said on December 1 of this year. "A gift for my love, every day. What could be better?"

Each year he stocks Gran's Advent calendar with daily treasures chosen especially for me. When I behold the childlike glow on his face as I open one of Gran's cabinet drawers, I'm reminded of what she always taught me about gift giving: for the pure of heart, the giving is greater than the getting.

On our second Christmas together, Juan and I added cookies to our seasonal ritual, baking together in our tight and tidy kitchen, decorating each cookie with sugar icing, though Juan's creations always come out prettier than mine. Once the cookies are iced and boxed, Juan dresses up as Santa and I as his elf, and we give a box to every neighbor we know in our run-down apartment building, leaving extras at the doors of strangers we feel could use some holiday cheer.

On our third Christmas together, Juan had a new brain wave.

"Our apartment window looks out onto the street. Some of the other tenants put up lights. We should, too!" he announced. Before I could stop him, he marched to the hardware store down the street, bought a set of multicolored twinkle lights, and installed them around our living room window, creating a blinking wonderland that could be seen from a mile away.

And then there was last year's tradition à la Juan, by far his wildest yet. On the day of the first snowfall in December, he burst into the living room, where I was sitting on our threadbare sofa, and said, "Let's take a ride in a horse-drawn carriage—jingle all the way! I've always wanted to do that—a romantic ride through the city streets with my Molly by my side."

"What a nice idea," I replied. "Let's look into it sometime."

"Look into it?" he answered. "Let's do it right now!"

And so I found myself bundled in a warm coat, Juan cradling a flask of spicy hot chocolate he'd brewed himself. Down to the city's main square we went, where the holiday carriages were circling. Juan's face fell when a driver told him the price of a short ride—far beyond our meager means. His hand went to his wallet, but I stopped him before he could pay. "Juan, it's too much money. Surely, there's something else we can do instead."

His eyes lit up then, and that devious little dimple on his cheek made an appearance as it always does when he gets an outrageous idea. "You're right, Molly. I have a better plan."

This is how I found myself back in the main square the day after. This time, I sat in a discarded children's sleigh fished from a dumpster by Juan Manuel, who was wearing an old fur coat that once belonged to Gran, dollar-store reindeer antlers on his head, and a red clown nose. He pulled me around the main square on the sleigh—twice!—and I laughed the entire time, as did everyone else who witnessed our silly, joy-filled spectacle. A photo of this moment sits on Gran's curio cabinet to this day. My head is thrown back in laughter, and Juan is looking back at me—expectant, jubilant, and maybe (I hope) a little bit in love. Who knew a reindeer could cherish a carriage ride so much?

Now, as I lie in bed struggling to sleep through the early Sunday morning hours, I watch Juan in the shadowy light, slumbering peacefully on his pillow. So many memories of Christmases past swirl in my mind. Soon, we will spend our fifth holiday season together—may it be as merry and bright as all the ones we've shared before.

Juan's face is soft and so dreamy sweet. Even though it's nearly eight o'clock, I won't wake him. Not yet. He deserves a good lie-in. He's been so tired lately. That man of mine never stops. He's always seeing to some chore or another, making sure everyone's okay—taking care of friends, family, colleagues, guests at the hotel, and me.

Yesterday, we worked a long day at the Regency Grand, me toiling in guest rooms as Head Maid and Juan doing double duty in the downstairs kitchen. He was promoted to Head of Pastry a couple of years ago. This means that during the holidays, he's in charge of many more preparations, all of them above and beyond his regular responsibilities.

When we arrived home after yesterday's shift, I was totally exhausted. I took my shoes off, wiped the bottoms, put them away in the front closet, then immediately flopped on the sofa in the living room.

"Good golly, Miss Molly," Juan said, eyeing me from the front entrance. "You're so *cansada.*"

"I am tired," I replied. "It's Christmas mayhem in that hotel. You must be exhausted, too."

He shrugged, then took off his shoes, wiped them down, and placed them neatly beside mine in the closet. A moment later, he was by my side, throwing Gran's lone-star quilt over me and planting a gentle kiss on my forehead.

"You rest. I'll cook us dinner."

I noticed then how dark circles had taken refuge under his lovely brown eyes. He looked so pale and worn out. I know he's working too hard, but he never complains, despite burning the candle at both ends. Sometimes, I think there's a lot on his mind, too, maybe more than I know. But what it is that troubles him, I couldn't say. He's not one to share his worries. Like Gran, he prefers to keep them contained and out of sight, hoping that if he does so, they'll simply shrivel from lack of light and cease to plague him. If only it were that simple.

"Juan," I said as he stood above me where I lay on the sofa. "You don't have to cook me dinner. You cooked for hundreds of people today at the hotel. We'll just have toast and tea."

"But it's Spaghetti Saturday!" he replied. "And it's date night with my tired but most dazzling princess."

He danced all the way to the kitchen then, throwing on Gran's old paisley apron and doing a little salsa spin in the threshold to make me laugh. It worked.

Spaghetti Saturday, Taco Tuesday, Huevos Wednesday. . . . For years, I've tried to convince Juan that I, too, can cook for us and relieve some of the burden in the kitchen, but he insists on doing it all himself, every meal laid before me as proof of his love.

"Molly, you clean from dusk to dawn. The least I can do is make our meals. Don't you know what they say about happiness? *La felicidad, así como el amor, entra por la cocina.*"

"Which means?" I asked.

"Happiness, like love, enters through the kitchen."

He started to hum then, disappearing amid a clatter of pots and pans. The sound lulled me, and before I knew it, I'd fallen asleep right there in the living room. I woke up only when Juan was by my side again, kissing my cheek and announcing, "*Princesa,* your dinner is served."

I peeled back Gran's quilt and groggily made my way to the kitchen, where the lights were dimmed and our worn wooden table was set with two heaping plates of spaghetti and meatballs. A lit candle between them cast a warm glow over everything, including the beautiful man in a paisley apron who was pulling out my chair for me and urging me to sit, eat, and enjoy.

And I do enjoy. Every minute of our lives together is a pure and simple pleasure. How I managed to be so lucky as to win this man, I'll never know. Sometimes, I wonder what I did to deserve him.

Last night, after dinner, I insisted on doing the dishes. Juan eventually relented.

"Fine," he said. "While you're cleaning up, I'll do some chores downstairs. And I'll pick up our mail."

He returned awhile later with a small package in his hands. "My mother sent something from Mexico," he said. "I wonder what it could be."

He opened the package as I looked on, removing a strange contraption from the envelope—a colorful braided tube made of dried palm leaves.

"*Ay, mamá,*" he said, laughing to himself. "I can't believe she sent one."

"What on earth is that?" I asked.

"Proof that my mother has ideas. And that she's very clever," he replied. "Come closer. Let me show you," Juan said as that devious little dimple made a reappearance on his cheek.

"Hold out your hand," he instructed.

I held it out.

"This is an *atrapanovios,*" he explained. "It's a kids' toy and a funny old Mexican tradition. The idea is that when you want someone by your side forever, you attach the *atrapanovios* to their finger. When I was a boy, I used to wonder why anyone would want such a thing. Now that I have you in my life, I completely understand. Here," he said as he slipped the silly-looking tube onto my finger. It held tight, and try as I might, I could not slip it off.

Holding the other end, Juan, with a goofy grin on his face, pulled me toward him until I was happily enveloped in his warm embrace.

"Looks like I'm stuck with you," I said.

"Exactly. That's the whole point. But if you don't want to be, that's okay. I just do this . . ." He pulled some hidden lever in the device, and the contraption fell loose around my finger. "See? Now you're free. What do you think?"

"I think you don't need a toy to keep me by your side," I replied as my hands found his cheeks. "My gran used to say, 'If you love something set it free.'"

"If it comes back to you, it's yours," he said, kissing my lips.

". . . and if it doesn't, it was never meant to be,'" I said. "So you have the saying in Spanish, too?"

"We do," said Juan.

Just then, I looked down at my left hand where it rested against Juan's chest. The *atrapanovios* had left a dark, chalky mark around my finger.

"Is it supposed to leave a stain?" I asked, holding up my hand to Juan.

"Uh, yes. All part of the fun!" he replied.

Before I could question him further, he suddenly let go of me, rushed down the hall to the bathroom, then raced back a moment later and said, "I have an idea! For Spa-ghetti Saturday!"

"But we had dinner already," I replied.

"Yes, but it's time to put the 'Spa' in 'Spa-ghetti," he said. "What about a relaxing and rejuvenating date-night excursion to a luxurious couples' spa—a bubble bath for two, right in the heart of the city?"

"Oh, Juan," I said. "You know we can't afford things like that."

"Ah, but we can," he replied. And again, he raced off down the hall, this time to the kitchen, returning to my side with a bottle of Sunlight dish soap in his hand.

Before I knew it, I was chest deep with Juan in our scuffed soaker bathtub as he counted and kissed each of the toes on my right foot while sporting a sudsy Santa bubble beard with a matching foam mustache.

We stayed in that tub, talking and giggling and telling stories, until our flesh was pink and pruned. Then, my beloved wrapped me in a fresh towel and meticulously dried me off inch by inch. I did the same for him, lingering as I sponged the terry cloth over his strong shoulders and across the vast expanse of his deliciously smooth chest.

Dried off, drunk with warmth, we ran to our bedroom with not a stitch of clothing on and collapsed into bed.

"I'll be right back," Juan announced.

"What are you doing now?" I asked.

I could hear him in the bathroom, cleaning out the tub, knowing it would bother me to find rings on it in the morning. He was determined to leave the entire bathroom spick-and-span, not for his sake but for mine.

I curled deeper into our bed, anticipating his return, breathing in the lemony scent of our bath together. And that's when I must have drifted off to sleep, only to wake early this morning. Juan must have tiptoed into bed beside me last night, careful not to wake me, though I would have relished feeling him wrap himself around me before both of us drifted off to sleep, at rest in each other's arms.

Now, as I lie in bed, a shadow from the curtain falls across Juan's serene face. I feel a sudden pang of despair, and I don't know where it comes from. Nothing in my life would be what it is without Juan, and I suppose I still struggle to comprehend why he's with me. I've felt this before, of course—this fear, this dread. I felt it when Gran was sick. I worried myself ragged about how I'd forge a life without her. And yet, here I am. I did it. But I don't think I could survive that kind of loss again. I don't know what I'd do without this man beside me, because no matter how much brightness he brings, I'm still so afraid of the dark. There is no *atrapanovios* strong enough to keep Juan with me forever. All I can do is hope that my love is enough.

These are the thoughts that make me spin and plummet backwards, traversing well-worn paths to the darkest of memories. I can't help but recall that first Christmas I spent alone without my gran. It was the most dismal holiday I've ever endured—a long season of sadness. It wasn't just the loss of her, the absence of carols sung in her cheerful voice, or finding each of the drawers of her Advent calendar empty of small treasures. It was the deep, abiding loneliness that surrounded me at work, the constant reminders that the social world was a mystery I couldn't solve without her.

The staff Christmas party at the Regency Grand is always a lovely event. Held in the lobby *en pleine vue,* it features mulled cider, tea, and Christmas cookies. I look forward to it every year. But that first year without Gran, the staff party was the only holiday festivity I was invited to, and that made it feel even more special than usual. Mr. Snow had the idea of doing a Secret Santa gift exchange amongst staff members, and I drew Cheryl's name, much to my chagrin. Still, I was determined to show her some holiday spirit.

The day of the party, all the staff gathered in the lobby—bellhops and bartenders, doormen and dishwashers, clerks and cooks. Everyone was festively dressed and full of holiday cheer. The Secret Santa gift exchange proceeded, with Mr. Preston handing out one gift at a time as the staff looked on. I was excited when he grabbed my gift for Cheryl and presented it to her.

But the second Cheryl unwrapped the brown paper, her face fell. "Eww. It's used chocolates from our turn-down service, shaped like a Christmas tree. So much for Secret Santa, Molly," she said with a guffaw.

"How did you know that gift is from me?" I asked.

"No one else is weird enough to regift discarded turn-down chocolates," she replied.

"They're not discarded. They're upcycled," I explained. "Waste not want not."

"Now, now," said Mr. Snow before I could say anything further. "Christmas is about kindness, a quality some here are rather short on." He eyed Cheryl, then bent to pick up another gift from under the tree. "Here, Molly," he said. "This one has your name on it."

The package he offered me was wrapped in gold-striped foil with a silver ribbon on top.

"Who do you think it's from?" I asked the staff members gathered.

"Dunno," said Rodney, the handsome bartender I was besotted with at the time. "They call it Secret Santa for a reason, right?" Rodney winked at me then, and not knowing at that point what a bad egg he was, I instantly grew weak in the knees.

"Open it, Molly," Juan Manuel said as the others watched.

I ripped off the wrapping paper to reveal an action figure encased in a cardboard and plastic bubble—Rosie the Robot from the old TV show *The Jetsons.* I was utterly perplexed. "But this is a child's toy," I said. "Surely this gift was meant for someone else?"

"Oh no," Rodney said with a chuckle. "It was definitely meant for you."

Like a virulent contagion, muffled laughter traveled from person to person. Receptionists hid giggles behind cupped hands. Valets chortled and elbowed each other. Even some of the maids I worked with every day tried hard to suppress their smiles.

I stared down at the toy in my hands. Roomba the Robot, Oddball Moll, the Formality Freak—all names I'd been called before by the people I worked with every day. The joke was on me, but I was not laughing. I felt so small, so foolish. I studied the sheen of my perfectly polished shoes.

"That's enough," Mr. Preston said as he tried to quell the laughter.

Juan Manuel sidled up to me. He laid a comforting hand on my arm. "My Secret Santa got me Earl Grey tea, Molly. Would you trade gifts with me? I'll send that toy to my nephew in Mexico. He'll love it. Upcycle, right? Waste not want not?"

I searched his face for signs that he, too, was mocking me, but his dark brown eyes were serious and glassy, his mouth downturned in an expression I could not have named at the time, though as I recall it now, I do believe it was compassion. "Thank you, Juan Manuel," I said. "That's kind of you."

"At least someone around here understands the Christmas spirit," Mr. Preston muttered under his breath.

"Hear, hear," said Mr. Snow.

I'm still in bed, wide awake, circling the past, searching for what, I do not know. It's been years since that Christmas, and yet my memory catapults me back. Try as I might to resist the pull, I sometimes get carried under.

The light is starting to break through our bedroom window. The clock on the bedside table says it's nine, and yet Juan remains sound asleep beside me. I can't remember the last time he slept this late on a Sunday; he's usually up at the crack of dawn, chirping away like a little songbird, singing a happy tune.

In the distance, bells jingle-jangle, with Christmas just around the corner. I listen to the rise and fall of Juan's breath as he slumbers. I love his long, curled eyelashes, which all the ladies coo over. In this cold weather, snowflakes catch on those beautiful lashes, framing his chocolate eyes in a rim of sugary white.

"You're my special snowflake," I told him just last week. We were holding mittened hands, making our way home from our shifts at the Regency Grand as the first snowfall gently alighted. I do realize that the expression "special snowflake" is meant as an insult. I should know. After all, it's one that's been directed at me more times than I can count, but I've chosen to transform it into a compliment, for what could be more precious than a snowflake, no two alike, each so perfectly, wondrously itself?

Juan's eyelids flutter. He adjusts his head on the pillow beside mine. Then his eyes spring open. A smile blossoms on his sleepy face. "*Mi amor,*" he says with a big stretch. "What time is it?"

"Precisely two minutes past nine," I reply.

"*Dios mío,* it's late!" he exclaims. "We must cease the day."

"Better yet, why don't we seize it," I reply. I lean forward and kiss each of his eyes. He pulls me into an embrace and plants a garland of kisses down my left cheek.

"What would I do without you, Mrs. Molly?" he says.

"Mrs.?" I reply. "That makes me sound much older than my thirty-something years."

"You are anything but old, *mi amor.* You are youthful and picture perfect in every way. You're the apples of my eyes."

"A veritable orchard then," I say, and at this we both collapse in laughter.

Juan folds me into him so that I'm resting on his smooth, bare chest. He grins, then pulls the covers up over our heads.

"You can't still be tired," I say.

"I've suddenly woken up," he replies. "You?"

"Wide awake. For hours."

His hands find my face, and he holds them to my cheeks as though reciting a silent prayer. Then he kisses me.

It's like this every time—I melt at his touch. There's a fire in me I never knew existed, one that ignites the second he lays his hands upon me. Somehow, he expels all shadows of grief and doubt that creep into my being with alarming regularity. He is my balm and my comfort. No one but him can so easily banish my worldly concerns. Before Juan, I had no idea that such a pure pleasure as this existed, that love could be expressed in this physical form. It is a delight I could never have dreamed of, a wonder for which I have no words.

Later, we rest in each other's arms as the light streams through the crack in the curtains. For once, the dust motes dance on the sunbeams and I have not the least inclination to clean them. Never in my life have I felt more content than in this moment.

Suddenly, Juan gasps out loud, and I almost jump out of my skin. "What is it?" I ask, my heart pounding.

"The Advent calendar! I almost forgot—today is a *very* special day."

"Juan, you scared me half to death. I thought there was some sort of emergency."

"Sorry," he says. "You know how excited I get about the Advent calendar. Come! I can't wait for you to see today's gift."

With that, he hops out of bed, stumbles into his reindeer pajama bottoms, and shuffles to the living room while singing "*Feliz Navidad*" at a decibel level that I fear may elicit noise complaints from our neighbors.

Alone in our bedroom, I make my way back into my matching reindeer pj's and smooth out my rumpled hair. I wonder what treat Juan has in store for me today. For a couple of weeks now, he's been thrilling me with daily delights, populating each index-card drawer with thoughtful trinkets and treasures. So far this month, I've received a silver thimble, an upcycled turndown chocolate from the Regency Grand, a green pet pompom named Frank (complete with googly eyes Juan glued on himself), some jingle bells, a fresh and festive dusting cloth, and a miscellany of other marvelous *objets.*

Once I'm properly dressed, I check myself in the full-length mirror on our bedroom door. My cheeks are unusually flushed. My sharp black bob is mostly back in ship-shape order, if not perfectly coiffed then at least acceptably neat for first thing on a Sunday morning. As I study myself, a dark shadow crosses my face. What does Juan see in me? I wonder. When he could choose so many others, why in the world would he choose me?

There's no one more precious in all the world.

It's Gran's voice I hear, and for a moment, I swear I can see her behind me in the mirror, her hands on my shoulders. But when I turn, she's gone. My eyes are playing tricks on me as they sometimes do.

I smooth out my bob one more time, then amble to the living room, where Juan has tuned in to Christmas carols on the radio; he's singing along, making up the words when he can't remember the real ones. He stands by Gran's giant Advent calendar, a Cheshire cat smile on his face and his tousled hair like a rooster's off-kilter coxcomb. He points to today's date on a drawer. "Open sesame," he says.

I approach and slide the drawer open. Inside is a snow globe, which I pick up and cradle in the palms of my hands. The scene within the glass orb takes my breath away. It's the Regency Grand in miniature, complete with two tiny figures poised halfway up the red-carpeted stairs.

"Where did you get this?" I ask.

"Mr. Snow was throwing it away," says Juan. "Apparently, these were made years ago to drum up special-events business at the hotel. Give it a shake, Molly."

I do so, and the globe swirls with white specks, turning the hotel into a magical wintry wonderland.

"Snowflakes!" I exclaim. "And look! There's a little tuxedoed doorman on one knee helping a woman in white up the stairs."

"Really, Molly?" says Juan. "Is that what you see?"

"Yes," I reply. "What do you see?"

"It doesn't matter," he answers. He turns away from me then, and for a moment I wonder if I've made some kind of faux pas because his smile has completely disappeared. But when he turns back to me, all is well again, his smile kind and warm.

"I should know better than to insist you see what I do, Molly," he says. "And besides, this is your gift, not mine. Do you like it?" he asks, pointing to the miniature world in my hands.

"I love it," I reply. "It's a treasure. And so are you."

He wraps his arms around me. "Tell me, Molly. What do you want for Christmas more than anything else?"

I consider this. Gran and I used to make long Christmas lists for each other, filled with impossible items that we could never afford or that simply didn't exist—a time-traveling unicorn; a luxurious rent-free apartment; education without school or bullies; endless clotted cream with scones. Buried amongst the impossible was the one item within reach.

"Tea towels?" I say now.

"Honestly, Molly." He looks at me with an expression that may very well be exasperation. "Can you dream just a little bigger for once? Please? If you could have anything in the world, what would it be?"

On the radio, a familiar singer croons a carol, offering the exact answer I hear in my head.

"All I want for Christmas is you," I say.

"Are you sure about that?" Juan asks. "You must tell me now—right now—if you're not sure."

"Of course I'm sure. I'm one hundred percent, absolutely and definitively certain," I say.

Juan lets out a massive sigh, then brings my hands to his face, smothering them with kisses. "The perfect answer from the perfect woman," he says. "Sometimes I wonder if I'm not understanding, like maybe I'm interpreting the cues wrong. Do you know what I mean? Has that ever happened to you?"

"You can't seriously be asking me that," I reply.

"Oh, I am," says Juan. "In fact, I'm more serious about this than I've been about anything in my entire life."

Chapter 2

Juan is in the kitchen making breakfast. As he does so, I locate the festive dusting cloth he gave me a few days earlier. I dust off Gran's curio cabinet, then polish the photos that sit on top in glowing gold frames. I position the Regency Grand snow globe between the photos, giving it a place of prominence between the people I have loved most in this world.

I can hear eggs sizzling in the pan in the kitchen as Juan sings along to "The Twelve Days of Christmas." We still have a few preparations to complete before the twenty-fifth, and we must get everything done on this final Sunday before the last short and busy workweek of the year. Then, on Christmas Day, Mr. Preston, my grandfather and the beloved doorman at the Regency Grand, will arrive at our apartment door with bells on—and to be clear, I mean that literally, not figuratively. Charlotte, his daughter, will be by his side, dressed in a Christmas-themed sweater and laden with so many gifts it's a wonder she will be able to carry them all.

It's not that I'm clairvoyant—this has been our tradition for a few years now, a happy Christmas of found family brought together by fate. And if the fates allow, we will enjoy another season *en famille* in just a few days. My only regret is that Gran won't be there with us, though sometimes I wonder if she is. Like the star atop a Christmas tree, perhaps she shines her light down on us from above. It's a thought that gives me comfort at this time of year.

And speaking of trees, that's on the to-do list today for Juan and me. We must buy a tree and decorate it—a real one, Juan insists, rather than the old artificial one we usually put up. Then we'll deck our halls with all the Christmas spirit we can muster. We're a little late this year, mostly because we've been working overtime and weekends at the Regency Grand. The hotel has been booked solid for weeks. We're lucky, in fact, to have this one day off together.

"Breakfast is ready!" Juan chimes from the kitchen. "*Chilaquiles para dos,* with tea and crumpets."

I head to the kitchen, where Juan—beautifully bare-chested but wearing Gran's old paisley apron—has laid two full plates at our kitchen table.

"*Buen provecho,*" he says.

"*Bon appétit,*" I reply, sitting down at my place across from him. Breakfast is as scrumptious as the tousle-haired man who serves it to me. Between hearty bites, Juan chatters about how many more Christmas cookies he and the staff at the Regency

Grand still have to bake and how this year he's overseeing not only the specialty holiday cookies but also the construction of the Ginger Grand, a replica hotel made entirely of gingerbread, jujubes, old fashioneds, humbugs, gumdrops, and enough sugar icing to induce a diabetic coma in every guest, though fortunately, the gingerbread hotel is for display rather than digestive purposes.

Once breakfast is finished, I bring our plates to the sink and begin the washing up.

"Oh!" says Juan. "I've just remembered. I need to quickly pop down to the laundry. You get ready for our Christmas tree adventure, and I'll be back before you can say 'Juan Manuel is the best boyfriend ever.'"

"Very well," I reply.

He kisses my cheek, removes Gran's apron, then hurries to our bedroom to grab a shirt. He's out our front door and heading to the building's basement laundry room before I can even remind him to take the hamper.

While he's gone, I do the dishes—washing, drying, and putting them all away. I expect him to return *tout de suite,* but he's still not back by the time I've returned the kitchen to a state of perfection. Perhaps he's decided to fold the laundry downstairs, though it's hard to imagine why. Mr. Rosso, the landlord and owner of our decrepit building, is more miserly than Scrooge himself. Recently, he removed nearly all the overhead lights in the laundry room in an effort to "discourage loitering," not that anyone in their right mind would spend a second longer than strictly necessary in that dark, spider-infested inferno. I've petitioned Mr. Rosso to reconsider his plan for greater lighting efficiency, raising the safety and well-being of tenants, and while I did not receive a formal response in return, Mr. Rosso's grunt, followed by a slamming of his front door in my face, left few doubts as to his true feelings on the matter.

Stand up for what's right or you'll sit on the sidelines all your life.

Gran understood. She had the door literally and figuratively slammed in her face—so many times over the years, and yet she always made the choice to shine light in the dark.

I dry my hands on my tea towel, then head to our front door, opening it to check for Juan. I look right and left down the long corridor, but there is no sign of him. No matter. I decide to take a shower, then get dressed in my favorite Christmas sweater, the one festooned with every Christmas ornament imaginable, including candy canes that light up (battery operated). I pair this with red-and-white-striped leggings. Once clean and fully clothed, I check myself in the mirror—perfection.

I head to the living room and settle myself on the threadbare sofa, waiting for Juan to return, which he does about fifteen interminable minutes later.

"Are you all right?" I ask the second he walks through the front door.

He looks piqued and overheated, like a glazed donut melting in the sun. Both his arms are smudged with grime, and though I didn't think it possible, his hair has achieved an even greater state of disarray.

"I'm fine!" he responds in his singsong voice. "Some issues in the laundry room, but all is well."

"Where are our clothes?" I ask. His hands are empty, no laundry in sight.

"Oh. I forgot. I brought everything up last night and put it all away. My mistake."

He removes his shoes, wipes the bottoms, then neatly stores them in the front closet. Next, he heads down the hall to the bathroom, closes the door behind him, and switches on the loud ceiling fan before I can ask what he was doing in the laundry room for so long if not the laundry.

I hear the familiar groan of the shower turning on, and above that, the whirring of the fan. Juan soon begins a Christmas concert solo in the confines of our bathroom, belting out "Joy to the World," followed by an especially jaunty rendition of "Deck the Halls." I know he's nearly done when he reaches the high part in "O Holy Night." The shower stops, then moments later the bathroom door bursts open, and Juan's bare feet pad down the hall to our bedroom.

I wander over and stand in the doorway as he gets dressed. Our soiled clothes hamper is where it always is, in the corner by the bed, but it isn't empty, as I expected it to be. Rather, it's three-quarters full.

Juan watches me from the bed as he wrestles socks onto his damp feet. "You're wondering what I was doing in the laundry room. An old lady needed help."

"An old lady," I say. "Mrs. Nguyen?"

"The woman down the hall? No, not her," he says.

"Mrs. Bancroft from the fourth floor?"

"Do you know her well?"

"Not really," I reply.

"Yes, it must have been her. Mrs. Bancroft," he says. He pops up from the bed like a gopher emerging from a smoke-filled hole, rushing toward me and sweeping me into his arms. He smells soapy clean and fresh, and at long last, his hair is neatly combed.

"Are you ready, Molly? It's time to choose our Christmas tree! I'm so excited."

He kisses me then, his mouth minty fresh, and I forget all about old ladies and laundry and just about everything else.

We don coats and shoes and head out the door. Holding mittened hands, we make our way out of the building and onto the sidewalk dusted with powdery snow. The Christmas tree lot isn't far away, just a few blocks. It's a pop-up installation set up once a year in a grocery-store parking lot. I swear I could make it there with a blindfold on just by following the scent of fresh conifers redolent in the air.

When we arrive at the lot, the burly tree seller heads straight to us. "Merry Everything," he says. "Need a tree?"

"We do!" says Juan. "Show us the best you've got."

"Look up," he replies as he points to a magnificent tree on display right behind us. It must be over two stories tall.

"We're actually looking for something a tad more modest," I explain. "Maybe my height?"

"Over here," he answers, walking us to the back of the lot. "I've got balsam fir, Fraser fir, Douglas fir, Norway spruce, eastern white pine, and one premium, deluxe option—beautiful blue spruce."

"Beautiful blue spruce!" says Juan. "That's the one for us."

"This way. Pick the tree you want. Let me know when you're ready." The man trudges off to help some customers gathered at the front of the lot.

"Are you sure we need a premium tree?" I ask Juan the moment the attendant is out of earshot. "Gran always said 'premium' is just a fancy way of saying 'foolishly expensive,' and I'm not sure we have the money to spare. The price of everything has shot up so much, you know."

"Christmas comes just once a year. And besides, how bad can it be?" As Juan says this, he checks the price tag on the nearest blue spruce. "*What?* This is insane. Are they all this expensive?"

We quietly check the tags on all the trees amassed in this far corner of the lot, which, I suspect, is where the cheapest options are collected.

When Juan finishes his price check, he stares at me, his expression one I've never seen conveyed quite so succinctly on a face before—the stunned look of sticker shock.

"Molly, we can't afford any of these trees."

"I know," I say. "But chin up, Buttercup. Where there's a will, there's a way."

I search out the man I'm looking for, who's easy to spot given he's wider and taller than anyone else on the lot and may very well be part tree himself. "Yoohoo!" I call out, and soon enough the burly lot attendant is trudging back our way.

"Which tree should I bind up for you?" he asks.

"Actually," I reply, "I'm afraid it is we who are in a bind—of the financial variety. We simply can't afford to purchase a tree at this price. Not this year, at least. I thought I'd ask if you have any budget-friendly trees that might be better suited to our . . . pecuniary predicament?"

"Uh . . . are you asking if I'll give you a tree for free?"

"No!" I reply. "Of course not. We're willing to pay, but at a more modest price point."

"I've got the Charlie Brown specials over there." He points to an evergreen pile beside a porta potty stall. "They're all bottom branches, so gnarly and bent I just hack 'em off the big trees. I could pound one onto a stand for you. Cost you a tenner."

"Sold!" says Juan.

The lot attendant grabs two thin pine planks and the mallet from his tool belt, banging them into an X formation onto which he spikes a spindly Charlie Brown branch. The "tree" has a ten-degree lean and several midlevel bare spots, but it sports copious pointy branches for ornaments and a lopsided coniferous tuft up top that reminds me of Juan's morning bedhead.

"It's perfect," I say.

Juan reaches into his back pocket and pulls out a bill to pay. "Thank you, sir!" he says as we leave the lot, our precious misfit tree tucked under his arm.

Chapter 3

Once upon a time, long, long ago, my gran recounted her rendition of a fairy tale featuring a princess and a frog. In her tale, a princess was sipping tea by a pond when her favorite gold-rimmed cup slipped from her hands. She watched in dismay as it glug-glugged down into the murky water, disappearing from sight. But no sooner did it sink than it reappeared on the shoreline in front of her, the delicate handle held awkwardly in the mouth of a muddy, misshapen frog.

"Did you retrieve that for me?" the princess asked the shiny amphibian.

"Yes," the frog croaked. "I've been watching you from these shorelines since I was but a tadpole. You are special. And kind. I would do just about anything for you. Here, take the cup. I know it's your favorite."

Ignoring the grime—though, to be clear, the princess loathed grime in all its myriad forms—she leaned forward and was about to kiss the frog's cheek in thanks, but before she could follow through, she heard a voice behind her.

"Don't touch that vile thing!" the voice commanded. "It's revolting."

She turned to see her betrothed, a strikingly handsome prince, standing by the edge of the pond, arms crossed, a petulant sneer on his thin lips.

"Are you coming with me, or would you rather roll in the muck with that repugnant creature?" he asked.

Gran paused in her story then, and for the life of me I could not understand why.

"What did the princess do next?" I prompted.

"She went with the prince," Gran said. "And by doing so, she made the single biggest mistake of her life."

"Why was it a mistake?" I asked. "The frog was covered in mud. He was filthy and vile. The amphibian was clearly a bad match for the princess."

"Was he?" Gran asked. "The frog was helpful and generous, willing to do anything for that princess, including wade through the mud for her. That frog had been watching out for the princess her entire life. Not everything is as it seems, Molly. We must learn to see past the grime, for what's beyond it may shine more brightly than any light you could possibly imagine. Remember that."

At the time, I could not quite grasp what Gran was getting at. Dirty versus clean, frogs versus princes, right versus wrong—it all swirled together in my head. "What happened to the princess afterwards?" I asked.

"Predictably, the handsome prince left her for a prettier princess. And when she returned to the pond to seek out the frog, he was gone."

My heart sank as she revealed the tragic ending, a rarity in Gran's stories. "But, Gran, this is such a sad tale."

"It is," she replied. "But it's only one chapter, with many yet to come."

"What's the moral of the story?" I asked.

"That a princess must discern wisely. Only this way will she ever be able to spot the difference between a frog and a prince."

"Molly? Molly? Are you listening?" asks Juan.

I've spiraled again, tunneling in my mind to a past that no longer exists. I'm having such a lovely time with Juan—right now, in the present. We're sipping hot chocolate from a pretty holiday stall set up on the sidewalk. I want to stay in the moment, and yet the past drags me under, miring me in silt from long ago.

Yesterday's the past, tomorrow's the future, but today is the gift.

"I'm so sorry, Juan," I say. "What were you saying?"

"I was saying, we've got our tree now. What if we pop into that jewelry store, the one on the corner? Maybe I'll find something for my mother. A necklace? Or a pendant?"

"But you mailed her a Christmas gift already," I say.

"I did. But it was small, almost nothing, really. Look at that," says Juan as he stops by a placard in front of the jewelry store. On the poster is a giant diamond bracelet on a woman's thin wrist.

"Diamonds are forever. This Christmas, give her the gift she really wants," Juan says, reading the slogan from the placard. "What do you think? Is that the gift she really wants?"

"It most certainly is *not,*" I say. What Juan has failed to notice is the fine print at the bottom of the poster, which I've actually read before on my way to this very store a few days ago. Gran always taught me to read the fine print very carefully. "Juan, do you realize that bracelet costs over ten thousand dollars?"

Juan squints at the poster, scanning the fine print for himself, our Charlie Brown tree quivering beneath his arm. "But the money's due in installments. That makes it better, no?"

"It doesn't matter!" I say. "What man would be daft enough to spend that much on a frivolity? You'd have to be a fool."

"A fool, yes. You'd have to be," says Juan as he takes a deep breath, then slings his free arm around my shoulder. "Oh, Molly. Sometimes, I love you so much, I worry I might go soft in the head. They say love makes people crazy."

"Please keep your wits about you. What use would you be without them?" I say as I pinch one of his cheeks. "Do you still want to go into the store?" I ask.

"No," he replies. "Let's just go home."

Chapter 4

Juan and I spend the rest of the afternoon in our apartment, decorating our misfit Christmas tree with popcorn garlands we make ourselves and all manner of baubles and trinkets collected from Christmases past. Even though it's only a rejected branch, it's remarkably sturdy and strong. As we decorate, it occurs to me that a Christmas tree holds so much more than ornaments. Resting on all those boughs is a treasure trove of memories that remain long after the tree is gone and Christmas itself is over for another year.

From the box of decorations at my feet, I gingerly pick up the miniature elf with legs like spindly green beans. Gran used to hang him high on the tree, claiming he kept watch over us, assuring that no harm would come our way during the holidays or in the year ahead. Reaching into the box, Juan removes an ornament in a wreath-shaped frame—a photo of his family assembled in three rows in front of a Christmas tree in Mexico.

He places the decoration at eye level so he can admire it every time he walks by the tree. His family is so far away, and yet they're near and dear to us, remembered every day.

After an hour of arranging, Juan and I are down to the final ornament, a bright star that Gran and I made years ago out of dry macaroni that we glued into an elaborate pattern and sprinkled with gold glitter from the dollar store. Juan places the star on top of the tree's funny evergreen tuft, where it twinkles in the late afternoon light.

He adjusts the topper several times to no avail. "I can't seem to straighten it. Our tree is horribly crooked," he says.

Years ago, such a predicament would have caused me great anxiety. A pit would have opened in the bottom of my stomach, rendering me as off kilter as the tree. But not anymore. I stare at the lilting evergreen with its akimbo star topper. "It's perfectly imperfect," I pronounce. "If I can lean into it, you can, too."

And Juan does exactly that. He leaves the leaning tree and comes to my side, taking hold of my hand, and for a moment we both stand there admiring the imperfection.

That's when there's a knock at our door. "Are you expecting anyone?" I ask.

"No," Juan replies.

I walk over to the door and peer out the peephole—a safety habit drilled into me by Gran when I was but a child. It's a stranger, a striking young woman about my age, with high cheekbones, feline eyes, and bouncy blond hair tied back in a ponytail. She's holding a long implement in her hand, but due to the distortion of the fish-eye lens, it's hard to tell what exactly it is.

"How can I be of assistance?" I call out as I keep watch through the peephole.

"I'm looking for the super," the woman says as she bats a wisp of blond hair out of her eyes. "I just moved in two weeks ago. Toilet's clogged again. Is he there?"

It's then that I recognize what's in her hand—a harmless plunger. I slide the dead bolt back and open the door.

"I'm afraid you've come to the wrong apartment," I say. "Mr. Rosso, the landlord, is just down the hall. That door right there."

Though I'm pointing very clearly to the door across the corridor, the woman pays me no mind whatsoever. Rather, she's fixated on what—or rather who—is behind me.

"Am I ever glad to see you!" she says, and when I turn, I realize she's talking to Juan. "My toilet's acting up again, and I can't figure out what the trick is. Any chance you can help?" she asks.

"I'm so sorry," I say to the woman. "Juan's a chef, not a plumber."

"A chef?" the blonde repeats, her nose crinkling up as though she's just sniffed the bell end of her plunger.

"I'm happy to help," says Juan. "Just give me a second."

Before I can say anything more, Juan saunters down our hallway toward the closet by our bathroom. He starts pulling out boxes and bins.

"You'll have to excuse me," I say to the plunger-wielding blonde. "My gran always advised me not to open doors to strangers, so . . ."

With that, I close the door in her face as gently as I can, then bolt it shut. I hurry down the hall to where Juan is rummaging through his toolkit.

"What are you doing?" I ask as he dons a tool belt and slips in various wrenches, pliers, and clamps.

He turns to me. "Aren't you always telling me to be kind to the neighbors?" Juan asks. "A clogged toilet this close to the holidays is a recipe for disaster. If it happened to us, we'd be distressed, too."

"But this is Mr. Rosso's issue, not yours. Don't you think he should handle it?" I ask.

"We all know where that will lead," Juan replies.

"Down the clogged drain," I reply.

"Exactly. This will only take a second. If I can't sort out the issue, I'll send her Mr. Rosso's way."

With that, Juan strolls down the hall toward the front door, whistling a little tune as I follow behind him. Once he arrives at our threshold, he stops, then turns to face me.

"Please tell me you didn't slam the door in her face," he says, eyes wide.

"Goodness, no," I reply. "I merely closed it in her face. These days, you can't be too careful. Stranger means danger, Juan."

"She's far from dangerous," Juan says. "And it's the season of goodwill and charity, remember? I'll be right back."

Juan opens the front door, and the blonde is still standing there. The minute she spots him, a look of relief blossoms on her face. "You're a lifesaver. Thank you!" she exclaims.

"Juan is very helpful," I say. "I'm sure he'll . . ." But before I can finish my sentence, Juan and the blonde are walking together down the hall toward her apartment.

I close the door behind me, leaning on it. There's something strange about what just happened, and as I think about it, I realize what it is: Juan seemed to know her. In fact, she seemed familiar with him, too. But how can that be if she recently moved into the building?

Be careful what you assume. Nothing is as it seems.

Of course. Gran's wise counsel reminds me not to jump to any silly conclusions. Who am I to begrudge Juan's kindness to a stranger, even if she happens to be an absurdly attractive one? It's not her fault she was born a natural beauty, nor is it my fault that I was born a . . . a what? A woman with mediocre looks that at best might be described as "natural," though unlike the blonde who was just at the door, I'm unlikely to win any beauty pageants.

Beauty is in the eye of the beholder.

Juan says the same thing whenever I put myself down, judging my looks and wishing to be prettier and more alluring than I am. Truly, while I don't know what he sees in me, I do know that one of the wondrous aspects of being human is that we appreciate different qualities in different people. I, for instance, love the fact that Juan's forearms and chest are smooth and bare, not a hair on them; that his left eye is slightly larger than his right; and that so often when he smiles, that mischievous little dimple alights on his cheek, a spritely divot containing a depth of delight.

A couple of weeks ago, that dimple appeared when Juan was

setting up Gran's Advent calendar in our living room. I patted his cheek the second I spotted it.

"What are you smiling about so fiendishly?" I asked.

"It's a secret," he replied as he fiddled with a drawer.

"But you're terrible at keeping secrets," I said.

"That's true," he replied. "But not this time. For once, my lips are sealed."

"But you know I don't like secrets. Please tell me," I begged.

"Not a chance," he answered.

"Then be careful," I cautioned. "My gran used to say that secrets have a way of punishing those who keep them."

"Not this one," Juan said as he closed another Advent calendar drawer. "This one will reward me. I'm sure of it."

Now, I wish I remembered which drawer he closed in that moment, because I would open it to see if it contained a clue to whatever mysteries he might be keeping from me. Maybe it wasn't the Advent calendar making him smile in the first place. Maybe it was something else entirely, a hidden thought locked in a private drawer in his own mind. If only I had the key . . .

I take one more deep breath and then stand up straight. I open our front door again to survey the hallway, and as I do, I spot Juan across the hall, conversing with Mr. Rosso outside his apartment. I close our door until it's barely ajar, leaving just a tiny crack that I can watch through.

Mr. Rosso's arms are crossed over his protuberant belly. Juan is explaining something to him but so quietly I can't make out all his words.

"You have to understand," Juan says. "Molly can't know."

"Your affairs are none of my business," Mr. Rosso replies with a snort and a flick of his nose.

"Thank you, Mr. Rosso. I appreciate your discretion," Juan says.

As I watch, Mr. Rosso offers a hand, and Juan shakes it. Or at least I think he shakes it, but then I see Juan slip something into his back pocket. Or is he just adjusting his tool belt? From this distance, I can't quite tell. Either way, I don't understand what I'm seeing. This exchange raises so many questions in my mind, I'm feeling dizzy. I click the door closed, and a few moments later, Juan opens it, nearly toppling me as he bursts in.

"*Madre mía,* Molly!" Juan exclaims. "What are you doing standing right by the door? I almost knocked you over."

"Sorry," I reply, "I didn't mean to get in your way." I step back to give Juan some space.

"Did you fix her pipes?" I ask.

"Fix whose pipes?" he replies.

"The beautiful blonde. Does her toilet work now?"

"Yes," he says, removing his shoes and wiping off the bottoms before placing them in the closet. "All I did was yank the chain."

"I see," I reply. "I'm pleased that's all she required."

I cross my arms against my chest, suddenly feeling cold.

"Molly, are you all right?" Juan asks. His eyes are wrinkled and tight, the left one larger than the other, as usual.

I look right into his eyes. "Do you know that woman?" I ask. "I can't make sense of why she showed up at our door out of the blue."

"Do I know her?" he echoes. He begins to fidget with the tools on his tool belt, his fingers running over them as though trying to locate some implement they cannot find.

"Yes. Do you know her?" I ask again, but I get no answer. "Let me rephrase: have you visited her apartment before?"

His eyes shift away from mine. "I don't really know her, Molly," he says, after a pause. "She was in the laundry room yesterday. She said hi. And I said hi. She knows which apartment I live in, I guess. That explains it, doesn't it?"

The truth reveals itself, the lie hides behind words. That's what Gran used to say.

I stare at Juan, and it's like his face is veiled. Usually, it's wide open, as easy to read as a picture book, but not now. I search it for clues, but for the first time in a long while, his face is an impenetrable mask. Suddenly, it's like I'm ten years old again, pleading for Gran's help at the grocery store because I have no idea if the cashier means to insult me or be kind.

Some things can't be explained. And some people are a mystery that can never be solved.

Chapter 5

After a long day of chores at home to prepare for the busy workweek ahead, my Sunday evening with Juan is over. I am past the odd incidents in the hallway with the strange woman and Mr. Rosso. As usual, I was probably overreacting and seeing things that weren't really there.

Just when I think I'm getting better at reading cues, life has a way of teaching me otherwise. For most people, it's easy to put two and two together, but not so in my case. I often get the sum wrong, adding the parts incorrectly or making more of the equation than it merits.

Juan and I went to bed hours ago. He's sound asleep beside me, the day ending just as it began. His breath is gentle—waves lapping the shore. Meanwhile, I'm wide awake again, though I'm quite tired. My mind is racing, searching shadowy corners and long-forgotten memories. I'm picking them up like boulders to see what lurks underneath, what answers will scuttle into the light.

The Sunday scaries. That's what Gran used to call this feeling. I have a serious case of them tonight, maybe because tomorrow is a big day—back to work at the Regency Grand during the busiest time of year, and our staff holiday party to follow the day after tomorrow. I really need to rest, and yet, here I am, staring at my beloved's face as he sleeps soundly on his pillow.

It takes me back to my teenage years. I used to lie like this, awake on a Sunday night, though no one slept beside me in those days. I dreaded Monday morning, which brought with it an unwelcome return to the classroom. Once there, I was either mercilessly scorned or ritualistically shunned by my classmates. Looking back, I'm not sure which was worse.

I do recall one day when I was genuinely excited to go back to school. It was right after the break for the holidays, and I vowed to start the New Year right—*New Year, New You,* just as the headlines proclaimed. Everything was going to be different that year—I was certain of it. I'd be the belle of the ball court, the queen of the classroom, the crown on the head of the entire student body.

That Christmas, Gran had given me a patchwork vest she'd sewn herself. It was brightly colored and hand-stitched, containing items of clothing that no longer fit me—my favorite blue jeans, a flowery blouse, even one of my old baby bibs with the slogan "Dinner's on me," a hilarious pun. In my youth, I found it hard to relinquish cherished clothing, even when I outgrew it, and this handmade vest was Gran's way of helping me let go of all the me's I used to be while preserving the cherished memories.

I wore that vest every day over the holiday break, and when the first back-to-school day of the new year rolled around, I couldn't wait to show it off to my classmates.

Elizabeth, the most popular girl in junior high, pointed me out the moment I walked through the school's front door. "That is seriously lame," she said, putting one hand on her hip and pointing the other at my vest.

Her gaggle of minions soon gathered by her side, doe-eyed and subservient. All of these girls whispered and laughed behind hands held tight to their mouths.

I decided to resolve things before they got worse. "I'll have you know," I said, "that the primary definition of the word 'lame' in most standard dictionaries is 'injured' or 'suggestive of a limp or similar impairment of gait.'" I stopped then, hoping for some engagement, but I was met by total silence. Naturally, I offered further explanation. "Perhaps you're confused by the word 'gait,'" I said. "I don't mean an opening in a fence or a passageway, I mean a way of walking—G-A-I-T, rhymes with 'wait,'" I said by way of clarification.

More silence. But when Elizabeth said, "Let's bounce," the girls by her side required no dictionary to grasp her meaning. They turned their backs on me in unison and bounded down the hallway in a cohesive clump.

Why does this memory come to mind now as I lie here listening to the ebb and flow of Juan's breath? My school days are long gone, and tomorrow I return to my work as Head Maid at the Regency Grand Hotel, a job I do not dread at all but perform with great relish and panache.

But for some reason, tonight, I feel more unsettled than usual, afraid of losing the safety and security that adulthood has bequeathed unto me. It's not fear of losing my work, which fills me with confidence and purpose, it's fear of losing Juan, of losing his love.

You belong where you're loved.

But what if I'm not loved, not really? What if I've read the cues all wrong, as I've done so many times before—mistaking frogs for princes, good eggs for bad? Much as I try to be affable and personable, I'm aware I can be irritating. I say the wrong thing at the wrong time, misunderstand what others grasp with relative ease. What if Juan loses patience with me? And what if what he really wants isn't me at all but someone, anyone else—like the beautiful blonde down the hall?

Your affairs are none of my business. That's what Mr. Rosso said to him. I'm sure I heard those words. They stick in my mind now like gristle between tight molars.

I turn, looking up at the white ceiling and counting the cracks in the dark. Is it my imagination, or is there a proliferation of new veins, conspiring to pull the plaster apart? How long before everything comes crashing down on my head?

I take a deep breath and close my eyes, willing myself to wring at least a little rest from this sleepless night. Eventually, feverish dreams descend. Juan sweeps me off my feet, whirling me around and around until I'm dizzy, repeating over and over again that he only has eyes for me.

"I don't believe you!" I insist. "Please, let me off the ride."

He puts me down then, and I hurry to our bathroom down the hall. In the mirror, I see myself, but I'm transformed, with three rows of bulbous, black eyes—pupil-less and dark. I'm still me, Molly, but the black widow version of myself, a spider so hideous, how could anyone ever love me? I scream at the top of my lungs, and when Juan opens the bathroom door, he screams, too, running out the front door of our apartment into the labyrinthine hallways of our building.

"It'll all be okay in the end!" I call to him. "If it's not okay, it's not the end!"

But he runs and runs, never looking back, until he disappears from my sight forever.

I want to cry, to let my feelings spill out, but my monstrous arachnid eyes don't allow for it.

"Molly? Molly? Wake up!"

My body jolts. Juan is lying beside me, his hair at right angles to his face.

"You were having a bad dream," he says as he strokes my forehead. "You kept saying 'eyes' over and over again. Are you all right?"

I look at the clock behind him—almost 7:00 A.M. Time to get up. "I'm perfectly all right," I say. "Just a silly nightmare."

"It's over now, Molly. You're here with me. Safe."

He takes me into his smooth, bare arms and pulls me so

close to his chest that I can hear his heart beating like a metronome.

Usually this sound soothes me—the pulse of life within him. But this morning, I'm unsettled by it. What if this isn't a life force at all but a countdown? What if my days with Juan are numbered and coming to an end?

Chapter 6

Once I'm awake for a few minutes, the bad thoughts retreat. It's like this sometimes. Terrible notions hold me prisoner in the night, removing all hope and seeding doubt deep within.

There are devils in the dark. Search for the light.

That's what Gran used to say. In the morning, she'd open the curtains in our apartment, and everything would look better when the light streamed in. I wonder now if she was plagued by bad dreams the way I was, if fear and anxiety overtook her at night, too. I wish I'd asked her that when she was still alive, but I was too young then, too fixated on my own devils to consider she might be contending with her own.

Now, Juan swipes the curtains open, then scoops me out of bed, giggling like a schoolboy as he carries me into the living room and puts me down in front of the Advent calendar. He stands impatiently beside it, hopping from one foot to the other, saying, "Open it! Open it!" Never in my life have I known anyone who loves gift giving as much as my beloved Juan Manuel.

I smile and slide open today's Advent calendar drawer. Inside is a little bundle of greens with sprigs of white berries. I recognize what it is right away.

"Mistletoe!" I say as I remove the sprig from the drawer.

"Yes!" he says. "And I already have a perfect spot for it, right above the kitchen entrance." He points to the passage, where I see he's affixed a little hook.

He takes the mistletoe from my hands and shuffles toward the kitchen, reaching up to place it high above his head. Then he strikes a pose underneath. "I figure if I stand under here long enough, you'll take the hint. Or at least the opportunity," he says.

"You are the silliest man I've ever known," I reply as I walk over to him.

"And? What else am I?" he asks.

"You are charming," I reply. "And thoughtful."

"Anything else?"

He leans on the entrance, waiting for more.

"You are perhaps a little bit handsome, even in reindeer pajama bottoms."

"You mean *especially* in reindeer pajama bottoms."

"Agreed," I reply.

"And therefore . . ." he says, looking up at the mistletoe.

"And therefore," I say, "I will kiss you."

I step closer and press my lips to his. His arms wrap around me, and the moment they do, all is right in the world.

We hurry through our breakfast; we shower and get dressed as quickly as we can. Then, we're out the door and walking briskly hand in hand to the Regency Grand, where a busy preholiday workday awaits us.

As we walk, Juan chirps away, filling me in on all the festive treats he's been learning to make. He's become quite a talented pastry chef, and his superiors have noticed. Gone are his days of toiling over the beast of a dishwasher in the steaming back room off the kitchen. Now, mixers and ovens are his domain, and he loves this new role.

"They're giving me more responsibility this year. I'm not only baking the Christmas cakes and cookies, I'm icing them, too. Do you know the difference between royal icing and fondant?" he asks.

"Educate me," I reply.

Juan launches into a detailed explanation not only of fondant and royal icing but of buttercream and marzipan, describing the full cornucopia of sweet delectables he's learned to create out of sugar. He talks so passionately that by the time we arrive at the front steps of the hotel, visions of sugar plums are dancing in my head.

But those are quickly replaced by a new and equally wondrous vision. The Regency Grand is decked out for the holidays, with garlands of holly winding up the brass handrails all the way to the gleaming gold revolving front doors. Tinsel festoons the doorman's podium, making it shimmer and glow in the morning light. Even Mr. Preston is wearing his holiday best—a long red greatcoat with a Santa hat in place of his usual doorman's cap. If I squint, I could mistake him for Father Christmas himself. He's chatting with an older couple, helping them carry suitcases and parcels up the stairs.

"Oh!" says Juan. "There's something I have to ask Mr. Preston. You go in and I'll see you later, Molly. Okay?"

"Sure," I say. I offer a little curtsy and he gives me his best formal bow. We both agreed long ago that kissing at our workplace would be the height of impropriety, so instead we avoid shows of affection when we're anywhere near the hotel, opting for formality instead.

Juan rushes up the stairs just as Mr. Preston returns to his podium, and I watch as he whispers in Mr. Preston's ear. They both look my way, and I wonder what it is they're whispering about. Still, there's no time to ask. I wave as I walk past them and into the hotel.

I'm delivered into the glorious lobby, which is at its most magnificent during the holiday season. The scent of cinnamon spice hits my nostrils—mulled cider is offered to guests at the reception desk, comforting warmth against winter's chill. The hotel staff don bell corsages throughout the month of December, which means the lobby rings pleasantly as valets, receptionists, and bellhops jingle-jangle across marble floors, luggage in tow.

But the lobby's pièce de résistance is the breathtaking Christmas tree beside the main staircase, a live evergreen so tall that only from the very top of the terrace are you at eye level with the tree topper—an elegant jewel-encrusted spire that casts an enchanting glow over both floors. Winding up the tree itself is a miniature Santa sleigh pulled by nine mechanical reindeer circling a snow-covered track from the bottom boughs right to the tippy top. Guests sit on the emerald settees, watching in wonder as the little sleigh spirals on its course up and through the tree, appearing a minute later at the summit, laden with wrapped gifts. There's nary a free seat in the lobby today as guests chitter and chatter, drinking mulled cider and planning their holiday shopping sprees.

"Molly!" I hear. I follow the sound to where our hotel manager, Mr. Snow—dapperly dressed in a forest-green velvet vest complete with a jingle-bell corsage—is waving at me from the reception desk. I walk his way.

"Just the person I wanted to see," Mr. Snow says, offering a demure smile. "I do appreciate your early arrival, Molly, especially as we're fully booked—and only a day away from our big staff party. Preparations are going well, but there's much more to do. The maids are bound to be quite busy upstairs today, too."

"Be a worker not a shirker," I reply.

"Touché," says Mr. Snow.

At regular intervals, groups of new arrivals stream through the gold revolving doors and into the bustling lobby.

"Listen, Molly," says Mr. Snow. "I've been thinking a bit more about our holiday party. I realize you're not a fan of the Secret

Santa gift exchange, and I wanted to check how you're feeling about the fact that we're doing one tomorrow amongst the staff." Mr. Snow eyes me in a curious way as he awaits my response.

"Perhaps you recall the Secret Santa debacle of Christmases past?" I say. "A few years back, your staff made me feel like an outcast on the very day when charity is expected. I will participate in the gift giving this year, but it's not like I've forgotten what happened before." What I keep to myself is that I've just relived that horrid event in my head, and I've no desire to recreate it IRL, as Juan would say.

"I do recall that dreadful occasion," Mr. Snow replies with a little sniff. "But that will never happen again. Not on my watch." To punctuate this, he removes his pocket watch from his green velvet vest. It is an antique timepiece, pure silver, with ornate, delicate hands.

"Careful!" I say as it slips from his grasp, as it so often does. I grab it just before it hits the hard marble floor.

"Good catch, Molly," Mr. Snow says. "Oh, and since you're here a bit early, could you have a word with senior managers and ask them to remind staff to bring their Secret Santa gifts to tomorrow's party? As I've explained to everyone, there's no need for extravagance. The theme is 'recycle and reuse.' If staff want to make gifts or regift items, not only will it be deemed perfectly acceptable, it will be lauded."

"Waste not want not," I say. "Put thrift in the gift."

"Precisely," says Mr. Snow.

"I do hope my Secret Santa likes my gift," I say.

"Whoever it is, I'm sure they will," Mr. Snow replies.

I try to stifle a smile so as not to reveal that the Secret Santa recipient I randomly drew is the very man standing before me—Mr. Snow himself. I'd hoped to select my friend Angela, the barmaid at the Social, or even one of the room maids I know so well. It would have been much easier to come up with a present they'd like, but alas, that did not come to pass. However, with a bit of thought and ingenuity, I'd figured out the perfect present for Mr. Snow.

"Is something humorous?" Mr. Snow asks, his eyebrows knitting together on his forehead.

"Not in the least," I reply as I return my face to neutral.

"Very well," he says with a little bow of his head. "You have my word that what happened to you the last time we did a Secret Santa will never happen again. Things will be different this year, Molly—I promise you."

"I appreciate that," I say as I hand Mr. Snow his pocket watch. "Be careful with this. Don't let it slip from your grasp."

"I'll do my very best."

I make my way to the basement change rooms in the housekeeping quarters. Inside, Lily, a marvelous young maid I hired last year, is already neatly dressed in her maid's uniform. She stands in front of a mirror, adroitly affixing her jingle-bell corsage above her name tag.

"Good morning, Lily," I say. "It's good to see you."

She smiles by way of reply but doesn't say a word, not that

this is out of character. Lily is the kind of person who speaks only when she has something important to say—unlike some. And by "some," I mean Cheryl, my least favorite maid on staff and the bane of my professional existence. Cheryl is splayed on a bench in front of her locker, flipping through the pages of a gossip magazine with a highly unsanitary licked finger. She's changed into her maid's uniform, but it is rumpled and disheveled. It's clear she's wearing the same uniform she wore on her last shift. Her freshly dry-cleaned one, wrapped in gossamer-thin plastic, hangs untouched from her locker door. I'm about to raise this hygiene infraction, but Gran's voice stops me.

Pick your enemies and battles wisely.

Cheryl is early for her shift (proving that wonders never cease), and given her fondness for tardiness and devious behaviors of all kinds, I must take this as a win. I breathe deeply, gathering strength. Then I pick up my own neatly pressed uniform hanging off my locker door and begin to change.

"Get a load of this," Cheryl says. "Marriage on rocks. Trouble in paradise!" she reads from the gossip mag she's been flipping through. She points to photos of a familiar celebrity duo on the center spread. The actor couple is well known to us at the Regency Grand. They stayed in our penthouse suite six months ago, causing quite a sensation. They seemed so happy at the time—newlyweds beaming in front of paparazzi lenses and joyfully signing autographs for guests and staff alike. But now, in these unauthorized photos, they're caught fighting in flagrante at their beachfront property in southern climes.

"Marriage is a sham," Cheryl says. "I wouldn't get married if you paid me."

"Are you sure about that?" Lily quips. She knows full well Cheryl's penchant for doing just about anything for money—including stealing tips meant for other maids. Lily catches my eye, and it's all I can do not to LOL, as Juan would say.

"Lily, if that clingy boyfriend of yours asked you to marry him, please tell me you wouldn't be stupid enough to say yes," Cheryl says.

Lily's boyfriend, Isaac, is devoted, not clingy—an upstanding young gentleman.

"I might say yes," Lily replies. She takes a brush from her locker and begins to smooth out her hair. "What about you, Molly?" Lily asks. "Would you say yes if he proposed?"

"Goodness, no!" I reply. "I have no interest whatsoever in Isaac."

Cheryl hoots with laughter, then wipes her nose with the back of her hand. "Lily, you're talking with Little Miss Literal. You gotta make things crystal clear," she says, pointing a germ-covered finger at me.

"What I mean," Lily explains, "is that if *Juan* proposed to you, would you say yes?"

I consider Lily's question as I finish getting dressed. I've done up the last button on my uniform and attached my jingle-bell corsage. Now, I add my favorite accessory—my name tag, which reads MOLLY, HEAD MAID.

"My gran used to say that a successful marriage requires falling in love many times. But the trick is that it's always with the same person."

Lily nods knowingly. "Yes. That's the trick."

What I don't say is that the last part of Gran's pronouncement gives me pause. Of course I adore Juan Manuel. There's no one else alive who makes me happier. Still, I'm not sure marriage is the key to assuring happiness will last. Gran never married, and she always warned me about making the wrong match, said it was hard to tell the difference between a good man and a bad one. *Fly-by-nights and wolves in sheep's clothing, Molly—some women become prey to them, learning the truth too late.*

"Ow!" I say, flinching as I inadvertently stab myself with my Head Maid pin.

"Careful or you'll stick that thing right through your heart," Cheryl says, her words sounding more like a wish than a warning.

"Oh, I almost forgot," I say. "Mr. Snow asked me to remind you to bring your Secret Santa gifts to the party tomorrow. And remember: recycle and reuse. That's this year's theme."

"Let me guess—that was your idea," Cheryl says as she sneers in my general direction.

"In fact, it was the brainchild of Mr. Snow—to discourage excess consumerism, reward thrift, and promote charity and thoughtfulness at this time of year."

"Not that you'd know much about that," Lily says so quietly I'm not entirely certain Cheryl hears.

"We'd best get going," I urge. "I presume the other maids are already upstairs?"

"They are," says Lily.

"I need to issue the same reminder to staff in the lobby, then I'll meet you on the fourth floor in a jiffy," I explain.

"I'll head up when I'm finished reading this article," Cheryl says.

"You'll head up *tout de suite,*" I reply. "The dream of clean works best as a team. Remember?"

Cheryl rolls up her magazine and jams it into her front pocket. "As if you'd let me forget."

Lily and Cheryl take the elevator to the fourth floor and begin cleaning guest rooms while I trot up the stairs to the lobby, heading straight for the Social bar and grill. Not only is my friend Angela the bartender but she was recently promoted to manager as well. Despite the big step up, Angela remains exactly the same—fiery as her flaming red hair.

"I'm up in everyone's grill. So what?" That's what she told Mr. Snow just the other day when he asked why she reprimanded the cook after he substituted smoked Gouda with processed cheese slices in the Social's signature sandwich, the Club Fromage.

"Standards, Snow," Angela argued. "You of all people should know how important it is to maintain them."

All of this was reported to me by Angela herself, complete with garnishes, side dishes, and an assortment of other verbal embellishments, because when it comes to Angela's stories, her appetite for explanation outequals my own. One thing I've been listening to quite patiently for the last few months is Angela's "five-year plan," to which she's sworn me to secrecy.

Angela's saving to go back to school to become a private detective. She's always been a true-crime aficionado, obsessed with criminal behavior. When that shady business went down a year ago and a famous author who shall remain nameless dropped dead—*very* dead—on the Regency Grand's tearoom floor, Angela's sleuthing powers proved helpful in solving the crime. Detective Stark, the investigator on the case, was quite impressed with her. And I suppose she was also impressed with me. In fact, Stark suggested *I* should retrain as a PI, but in truth, I think Angela's much more suited to that career. I prefer to clean rooms rather than crime scenes. Still, I'm excited about Angela's top-secret plan, and I look forward to living vicariously.

There she is now, batting an errant strand of red hair from her eyes as she pours two glasses of fresh-squeezed orange juice on a tray for a waiter standing by.

"Table two, be quick about it," Angela tells the waiter, who rushes off with the drinks. "Molly! What are you doing here? Shouldn't you be upstairs?" As she says this, she looks behind her into the storeroom entrance.

"Mr. Snow sent me on an errand," I say. I launch into my reminder about the Secret Santa tomorrow.

"Oh, don't worry. I won't forget to bring my gift," Angela says. "Would you believe I drew Cheryl?"

"So much for *Secret* Santa," I say, though if Angela catches my admonishment, she doesn't show it.

"I figured out the perfect gift for her," Angela replies.

"What?" I ask.

"A lump of coal. Or something worse if I can fish it out of my toilet."

"Now, now," I say. "It's Christmas, remember? The time of year to be generous and charitable."

"Even to those who don't deserve it?"

"Especially to them," I say.

Just then, a streak of red and white flashes through the doorway behind Angela—someone running full tilt toward the Social's back door. It happens so quickly, I barely have time to take it in, but if my eyes don't deceive me, that flash was my very own Juan Manuel in his white chef's uniform, carrying a huge bouquet of red roses.

"Did you see that?" I ask Angela.

"See what?" she asks, her fingers fiddling with her apron strings.

"Someone just ran through the storeroom behind you."

"No," she says. "I don't think so. I didn't see anyone." There's a look on Angela's face that's very hard to decipher. She makes a futile attempt to arrange her restless hair, which as usual refuses to respect the boundaries of her hair tie.

"I think it was Juan Manuel," I say.

"It can't be," Angela answers. "Why would your boyfriend be here instead of downstairs in the kitchen? You're seeing things."

"Someone was just there. I swear."

Angela begins to aggressively scour spots from a glass while I make my way around the bar to stand beside her.

"What are you doing back here?" she asks.

I ignore her, walking straight into the storeroom toward the rear exit, Angela nipping at my heels.

She ducks in front of me, then blocks the back door. "See?" she says. "Look around. No one here."

Indeed, the room is filled with bins and boxes, beer kegs and crates, but there's no one in it except us.

"Excuse me," I say as I sidle past Angela and push the long metal handle of the back door. I peek outside, looking left and right into the short alleyway out back—not a soul in sight.

I come back inside, shutting the door tight behind me.

"Honestly," says Angela. "You should get your eyes checked. Professionally."

I suddenly feel daft and ridiculous. Why am I chasing shadows that don't even exist, and what did I think I'd see outside that door?

"I don't know what got into me," I say. "Looks like I'm seeing things. Sorry. I best be off. Guest rooms don't clean themselves."

"Catch you later?" Angela says, and I nod, making my way to the bar, then leaving through the front entrance of the restaurant without looking back.

Only when I'm halfway through the lobby standing by the gold revolving doors do I spot the red-and-green smear on the palm of my hand. The handle of the Social's back door was sticky when I opened it, and whatever was on it is now stuck to me.

I hold my palm up for closer inspection. I sniff—the scent is sugary and sweet.

It may be fondant or royal or buttercream, but one thing is for certain—the sticky smear on my palm is icing . . . which means, contrary to Angela's assessment, my eyes don't require professional attention after all.

Chapter 7

I scrub my hands in the lobby washroom to remove the icing caked on them. *Out, damned spot.* The phrase repeats ad infinitum in my mind.

As I stare into the flow of tepid water, I remember how some time ago, a hotel guest used a word I was unfamiliar with, and when I later asked Angela about it, she said it had nothing whatsoever to do with electrics. The word was "gaslighting."

"It's when someone messes with your mind, makes you question reality," Angela explained.

Now, as I scrub out this red-and-green spot, her words return. Isn't that precisely what Angela just did to me—gaslighting? She made me doubt myself, question what I saw with my own two eyes—Juan Manuel, running full tilt out the back door of the Social with a big bouquet of red roses.

But why? Why would she pretend he wasn't ever there?

A thought crosses my mind, but I banish it before it can take root and spread like a contagion. Not only is it absolutely improbable that Juan was at the restaurant, but it's equally improbable that he was there to see Angela.

Or is it?

Juan often asks about her. "Did you see Angela today?" he'll query on our way home from work. "Have you spoken to her on the phone? How's she doing?"

I always fill him in on this or that, the most recent true-crime podcast she told me about or some shocking turn of phrase she used that made me BOL—blush out loud. I've always interpreted Juan's interest in her as friendly, a natural extension of caring for someone near and dear to me.

"Never in my life have I seen anyone with hair the color of flames—and a personality to match it," Juan said the other day when I was talking about Angela. I thought nothing of it at the time, least of all that he might find her attractive, which she most certainly is. But now, I have to wonder . . .

When you assume, you make an A-S-S out of U and ME.

It is absurd. I will give this notion no further thought. I will wipe it clean from the slate of my mind.

I pump the soap dispenser until my fingers are thick with lather, then I scrub my hands one final time. I wash the soap off, then dry my hands. But before I can head upstairs and resume the job I'm best at—cleaning up messes I can actually see rather than those streaking past into obscurity—I have one more reminder to issue, to Mr. Preston, the doorman, a.k.a. my gran-dad.

* * *

"Molly, my dear!" Mr. Preston says the moment he sees me. I'm standing on the red-carpeted stairs outside the main entrance of the Regency Grand, hugging myself against the mid-December chill.

"What are you doing outside? And without a coat?" He rushes over, about to remove his Father Christmas greatcoat, when I stop him.

"I won't be out here long. Just running an errand for Mr. Snow." I remind him of tomorrow's Secret Santa gift exchange.

"I, for one, am glad we're reviving that old tradition," he says. "Mark my words, it will be a memorable holiday party this year, Molly, with lots of surprises."

"Speaking of surprises, don't tell me who you picked," I say.

"I won't," Mr. Preston says, "but I do have a question for you regarding a gift for a very special lady."

"Very well," I say, pleased that he's taking pains to hide the identity of his Secret Santa recipient.

He reaches into his greatcoat and pulls out something shiny and gold from deep within, holding it in his enormous, bear-like hand.

"It's a Claddagh ring, Molly. Have you seen one before?"

I gaze at the lovely ring nestled in Mr. Preston's palm. It's a gold band with a heart in the center, held in place by two tiny hands. On top of the heart is a crown that catches the light, sending hopeful beams radiating out.

"My goodness, it's beautiful!" I say. "Did it belong to your wife, Mary?" I ask. Mary, a lovely woman and a good friend to my very own gran, died many years ago.

"It did not," my gran-dad replies. "I bought it long before Mary was even in the picture, and in the end, it has remained tucked away in a box all these years. Best that it sees the light of day, don't you agree?"

"I completely agree," I reply. "But it sure is extravagant," I add. I can only imagine the lucky lady at our Christmas party who opens her Secret Santa gift to discover this treasure is hers.

"It's interesting, Molly," he says. "Not everyone would appreciate this ring the way you do. From what I gather, these days young ladies prefer things modern and new, fresh from a fancy store. But I've always loved this old ring, simple though it is. Are you sure you like it?"

"Of course I like it," I say. "But that doesn't really matter since it's not for me. My gran always taught me to give a gift for the other person, not for yourself. That's real generosity, don't you think? And the true spirit of Christmas, too."

I wait for my gran-dad to answer, but he doesn't, and when I look up at him, I'm not quite sure what I'm seeing. Is it the cold, or are those tears welling in his eyes?

"Are you all right?" I ask.

"Never better," he replies. "Now remember, this chat we just had, it never happened."

"Of course," I say with a wink. "Your Secret Santa is safe with me."

Chapter 8

At last, it's time for me to do the job I'm meant to do—clean hotel rooms. I take the elevator to the fourth floor, where Lily is returning suites to a state of perfection. She's not engaged in this endeavor alone—Cheryl's with her—but the one thing Cheryl excels at is doing very little, which is why I must check in with Lily before anything else.

There's Lily now, dragging two enormous bags of soiled sheets into the hallway toward the housekeeping vestibule.

"Oh, Molly. Thank goodness you're here," she says. "I'm falling behind already."

"Not to worry. We'll catch up in a jiffy. I'll deal with Cheryl," I say.

"Thank you," says Lily, with an audible sigh of relief.

"Where is she?"

"'Taking a load off.' As usual." Lily points to a guest room at the far end of the floor.

I make my way over to where Cheryl's trolley is propping the door open. The moment I enter, Cheryl pops up from an easy chair and brazenly attempts to stuff her gossip magazine under the mattress of the unmade king-sized bed.

"I was just—"

"Shirking," I say. With Cheryl, it's best to interrupt the lamentable excuses before the offense to my ears becomes intolerable.

Cheryl has been on thin ice ever since she was caught last year handling hotel items that didn't belong to her. While Cheryl wasn't exactly penitent about her cleptomaniacal tendencies, I'll admit I took pity on her and petitioned Mr. Snow to give her a second chance to prove herself worthy of a job. And she's shown . . . mediocre improvement since then. But let's just say there are times, including now, when I regret my inclination toward mercy.

"Might I ask," I say, "how you intend to make up for leaving Lily in the lurch, cleaning rooms by herself all morning?"

As I say this, I remove the magazine Cheryl stuffed under the mattress and hand it back to her.

"I'll finish the rest of the rooms on this floor while Lily takes a long lunch," Cheryl says. "Fair and square, the maids all share."

She's quoting from *A Maid's Guide & Handbook*, a set of rules I developed to codify proper conduct amongst Regency Grand maids. I'm pleased that, for once, she's spouting something other than stories from her gossip rags.

Just then, a familiar sound echoes through the hallway—

someone singing along to "Have Yourself a Merry Little Christmas." I poke my head out the door, and Cheryl does the same. Both of us scan the hallway for the source of the sound.

"Oh look, it's Señor Dishy," Cheryl says.

My hackles go up instantly. "You mean Juan Manuel," I reply.

"I mean your lover boy, the dishwasher."

"The pastry chef," I offer by way of correction. "He was promoted as a reward for his hard work and loyalty—something to think about."

"Loyalty? You sure about that?"

As we both look on, Juan knocks on a guest's door, and a female patron dressed only in a bathrobe comes slinking out to greet him.

"Am I ever excited to see you! Especially after your special delivery the other day," she says with a wink. "Come in! I've got a little something for you . . ."

As I watch, dumbfounded, the woman grabs Juan Manuel by the arm and pulls him into her room. The next thing I know, the door slams closed behind them.

"What was it you were saying about loyalty?" Cheryl asks.

"Best get started on the bed," I reply. "Strip it bare and put on fresh sheets." I grab clean ones from the trolley and thrust them at Cheryl.

Normally, I'd help her make the bed, but a vertiginous sensation has overcome me, and I'm struggling to remain upright. My entire equilibrium has been thrown so off kilter I fear I may faint right in the open doorway. I peek down the hall one more time and see Juan emerge from the mystery guest's room, the door clicking closed behind him. He folds a few fresh bills in half and stuffs them into the breast pocket of his chef's uniform. Then he saunters down the corridor humming "I Saw Mommy Kissing Santa Claus" and acting like entering a woman's hotel room is the most quotidian thing in the world.

Cheryl throws the fresh sheets on top of the bed, then joins me again at the lookout spot. "Men," she says, once Juan is out of sight. "Just when you think you know them, they make you question everything."

"Best not to jump to conclusions. I'm sure there's some logical explanation," I say in a voice so unnatural I sound like a braying donkey.

"Oh, there's an explanation all right," Cheryl says. "Here." She hands me her magazine, flipped open to an article with a headline that reads: 3 SUREFIRE WAYS TO KNOW IF HE'S CHEATING ON YOU.

I don't want to read this rubbish, but my eyes have ideas of their own.

#1. *Does your boyfriend disappear and reappear with no explanation?*

Once yesterday, and twice today.

#2. *Is he tired all the time? Cheating takes energy!*

The dark circles under his eyes, the sleeping in when he's never done so before.

#3. *Does he give you gifts out of guilt?*

Every single day. The Advent calendar, each drawer filled with a new and exquisite treasure. I thought it was generosity, but what if it's something else entirely?

The floor beneath my feet starts to tilt again. I push Cheryl's magazine back into her hands and grip the maid's trolley in an effort to remain upright.

"Most princes turn out to be frogs in really good costumes," Cheryl says, her lips curling into a smile bereft of all joy.

"It's time for lunch," I say. "I need a break."

"Good idea," says Cheryl. "Let's take a load off."

She ambles over to the chair by the king-sized bed and flops down on it, licking her finger and turning the pages of her trashy magazine. For the first time ever, I don't have the strength to do anything about it.

Somewhere deep in my chest, my heart protests. I hear it pulsing all the way to my ears, feel it pounding against my rib cage—an empty cup clanging against iron bars. Dear heart, there is no escape—that's what I tell it, but the message isn't getting through. The futile protest continues.

I always believed this: that love was a safe haven, a refuge for those lucky enough to find it. But what if I was wrong? What if love is actually a prison with no escape?

Love is the greatest gift of all.

I head downstairs to the housekeeping quarters, where I grab my coat from my locker, ignoring the paper bag lunch, which Juan made me in the hotel kitchen. He does this every day, makes me lunch, then slips the bag onto the shelf in my locker while I'm cleaning rooms upstairs.

I can't eat, and I don't even want to think about the contents of that paper bag, with a note tucked inside as usual:

> *Sweets for my sweet. Love Juan*
>
> *You are the butter on my bread, the cheese in my sandwich. Love Juan*
>
> *Just a few days away from a Molly Jolly Christmas! Love Juan*

I put on my coat, then tromp up the stairs to the lobby. Cinnamon spice assaults my nostrils the second I ascend the final tread. The Christmas tree, so majestic just a few hours ago, suddenly looks sinister. It's only a matter of time until its needles drop and it's hauled to the curb—used up, discarded forever. Does this same fate await me?

Think the best, not the worst.

I'm doing it again, jumping to conclusions, rushing ahead before I really understand what it is that's happening. Juan deserves the benefit of the doubt. I must speak to him as soon as possible, once we're done with our shifts for the day. I must tell him what I've witnessed, ask him directly what he's been up to. Surely there's some explanation, some obvious facts I've managed to misinterpret.

Keep calm and carry on.

I march through the lobby and the cliques of jubilant guests vibrating with Christmas cheer and make my way out the revolving front doors. I rush down the red-carpeted steps before my gran-dad can stop me. I have an errand to run, and the fresh air will clear my head.

It takes eighteen minutes of brisk walking until I'm standing in front of the jewelry store that Juan and I walked by just yesterday. I pull open the door and walk in.

A pretty shopkeeper wearing a festive, form-fitting dress recognizes me right away.

"Oh, you're back to pick up your custom piece, right?"

"I am," I reply. "Is it ready?"

"It is," she answers.

She retrieves a small box from inside a cabinet, then opens it for me on the glass countertop. "Here it is. It was a simple adjustment—just a matter of changing the clasp to a T-bar."

"So the price you quoted me remains the same?"

"Yes," she replies. "Just ten dollars."

"Oh, that's excellent," I say. "Thank you." I take a bill out of my coat pocket and place it on the counter.

The shopkeeper looks at me, squinting, her head cocked to one side. "Weren't you outside our store just yesterday? I saw you with someone, but you didn't come in."

"Yes, that's right," I say. "I was with my boyfriend. He wanted to come inside, but after reading the fine print on your advertisement out front, I dissuaded him. My gran always told me it's dangerous to have expensive taste without a wallet to complement it."

"At least your boyfriend wants to buy you nice things," the shopkeeper replies. "You should count yourself lucky."

Usually, I do count myself lucky. But today, I'm filled with doubt. And for the first time in a long time, I'm no longer sure I'm so lucky after all.

Chapter 9

I return to the hotel with scant minutes to spare before the official end of my lunch hour. I rush up to the third floor, where Sunitha and Sunshine, two long-standing maids whose work ethics are as spotless as the guest rooms they clean, are finishing off the last few rooms on their roster. Sunitha and Sunshine require almost no oversight from me, and during busy times at the hotel, I know I can count on them to pull much more than their own weight. The proof is in how many rooms they've cleaned in just a few hours—and in how many tips they receive from grateful guests who appreciate their good work.

Sunshine and Sunitha are pushing their trolleys down the hall. They wave the moment they spot me.

"Molly!" Sunshine says with a smile as we meet in the corridor. "It's almost Christmas, and tomorrow's the holiday party."

"Yes," I say. "So it is." But I'm unable to rally excitement, so distracted am I by everything that's happened today.

"Molly, are you okay?" Sunshine asks, her eyes meeting mine. "Is something wrong?"

Sunitha then moves in beside me, too, concern writ large on her face.

"Have you ever had a day when everything turned upside down and backwards out of nowhere?" I ask them. "When everything you knew—or thought you knew—suddenly seemed uncertain?"

"Oh, Molly," says Sunshine. "Everyone has days like that."

"The good thing about bad times is that they pass," Sunitha adds.

I attach myself to this thought, and for the rest of the afternoon, Sunitha, Sunshine, and I work together, returning every room on the third floor to perfect order. Sunshine talks nonstop, and yet I register little of what she says. The work takes on a repetitive flow, and I'm lost in my thoughts, so much so that if you asked me which room I was in at any given moment, I wouldn't be able to say—the sheets, the beds, the sinks blending into one interminable blur.

The hours go by, and before I know it, it's five o'clock and our work is done. My dear maids have helped me through the day as they so often do. I curtsy and say goodbye, then head down to the change rooms, where I peel off my uniform and don my civvies once more.

I head up to the lobby and out the revolving doors, where I stand on the red-carpeted stairs and wait for Juan Manuel so we can walk home together. Gran-dad is on the sidewalk at the foot of the stairs, occupied with guests leaving the hotel. Just then, I feel a hand on my arm. I turn to find Juan Manuel, with his brown eyes and his enviable eyelashes, smiling at me.

"Brrr," he says as he pops the collar of his coat up around his neck. "Is it me, or has it gotten colder?"

"Frigid," I say as I pull my arm away from his.

His head tilts to one side as if he's a curious puppy. "Shall we walk?" he asks. "We'll be cozy once we make it home. We'll light up our Christmas tree, and I'll make us hot chocolate."

We head down the blood-red stairs and begin our trek back home in silence. When we're out of sight of the hotel, Juan tries to grab my mittened hand, but I cross my arms against the cold and continue walking.

"How are you, Molly?" Juan asks as we trudge along. "I bet you're tired. It's crazy busy in that hotel. I can barely keep up."

"Too many guests to service?" I ask as I search his face for some twitch or tic that might betray an iota of guilt, but all I see there is confusion.

"It's not just the guests, it's our own staff, too," he replies, "so many details to take care of for tomorrow's party. Are you looking forward to it?"

"I don't know," I say. "I'm not sure what to feel anymore."

"Are you worried about your Secret Santa gift? If you need something to give, I made a few extra batches of Christmas cookies today. I could box some up for you to give as your gift."

"No, thanks," I say. A niggling thought occurs to me. "Whose name did you pick for Secret Santa?" I ask.

"If I told you that, it wouldn't be a secret anymore, would it?" he says as he playfully wraps an arm around my neck.

"It seems I've misjudged you," I reply.

"In what way?" he asks, stiffening.

"I always thought you were terrible at keeping secrets. I see now how wrong I was. If you're not going to tell me who you picked, I won't reveal who I picked either. How does that feel, Juan, to have a secret kept from you?"

His arm alights from its perch on my neck and drops heavily to his side.

The rest of our walk passes in silence.

When we arrive home, Juan attempts to change the mood by striking up a merry rendition of "Jingle Bells." After wiping his shoes and putting them in the closet, he heads straight for our Charlie Brown tree to turn on the lights.

Just a day ago, the sight of our little misfit tree, all lit up, filled me with warmth and comfort—*home sweet home.* But now, when the lights turn on, the tree looks pathetic and misshapen. Even the macaroni star topper fails to enchant.

Juan busies himself in the kitchen, and soon enough he joins me on our threadbare living room sofa, where I've wrapped myself in Gran's homemade lone-star quilt. He passes me a cup of hot chocolate, but when I try it, I scald myself.

"Careful!" he says. "You don't want to get burned."

Too late for that, I think to myself, though I don't say it out loud.

Juan takes my cup and rests it on the side table beside his

own. "Molly, is something wrong? You can tell me, you know, if something's bothering you."

I wrap myself tighter in Gran's quilt, but it fails to bring me warmth. This is my chance to ask, to find out if my beloved has been gaslighting me all this time. "I have a question for you," I say, "and if I ask it, I want you to swear on your life that you will answer honestly."

Juan sidles closer and puts a hand on my quilted knee. "*Mi amor,* do you not know me by now? Of course I'll tell you the truth," he replies.

"Cross your heart and hope to die?"

He crosses his heart, then awaits my question.

"Were you on the fourth floor of the hotel today visiting a woman in her room?"

Now it's Juan's turn to flinch as if he's been scalded. He withdraws his hand from my knee. "Who told you that?" he asks.

"Cheryl saw you," I say. What I don't say is that I saw him, too, with my very own eyes.

"Since when do you trust anything Cheryl tells you?" Juan replies, but I'm not really listening to his words because he's grabbed his mug of hot chocolate and is walking away from me into the kitchen. My gran always said that if you want to know where someone's going, watch their feet, not their mouths. As Juan retreats and pours his beverage down the drain, I see the truth in Gran's words.

He reappears a moment later under the mistletoe in the kitchen entrance. He has yet to answer me. Does he really think his fancy footwork will get him out of this? Little does he know, my interrogation is not over.

"I have another question," I say.

"Go ahead," he replies.

"How do you feel about Angela?"

His face lights up the second I utter her name. "Oh, she's wonderful. I've been getting to know her better lately. She's very helpful. And I really like her. But you know that," he says.

"I do now," I reply.

Suddenly, something in me feels about to break. My stomach hollows out as if I've been punched. I can barely draw a breath. There's so much more to say, and yet I can't probe any further because my heart can't take it. I fear the answers I hear might mark the end of me. And more than anything, I worry the man in front of me is changing so quickly I hardly recognize him anymore.

"Molly?" Juan says from the doorway. "Do you have any other questions?"

"Just one," I say. "Have you heard of the silent treatment?"

He nods, then comes back to the sofa and sits beside me. "Isn't that when someone decides to punish you by not saying anything? It probably works well on people who talk a lot. Chatty people don't enjoy the silent treatment at all, am I right?" He stares at me, awaiting my agreement. "Molly? Am I right?"

I don't answer.

His face falls like a cake removed from the oven too soon. "Oh, I see," he says. "I guess this means you're not talking to me right now."

I don't say anything. Not a word escapes my mouth.

"But, Molly, we never argue. And whenever we disagree, we always talk about things to find a resolution. Teamwork makes the dream work, right?"

He's read my *Maid's Guide & Handbook to Housekeeping, Cleaning & Maintaining a State of Pinnacle Perfection* so many times his bedside copy is dog-eared and worn.

I suddenly feel so tired. Maybe if I close my eyes, I'll wake up and see the world clearly again. Maybe everything will go back to the blissful way it once was.

"I need to rest," I announce. "I'm going to lie down."

"Of course," says Juan. "You've had a long day."

I stand and make my way down the hall, Juan following close behind, but when I veer away from our bedroom, about to turn the knob to enter the other room, Juan stops me.

"Wait," he says. "You're going to lie down . . . in there?"

By "in there," he means in Gran's old room. I rarely go "in there." Her bedroom is a shrine, kept exactly as she left it when she died several years ago. I enter to clean and dust once a week, but otherwise, it's a door I prefer to keep closed. Except now.

I turn the knob and enter. Juan stands in the hallway, watching me tentatively.

"I need to be alone," I say. In all our years together, I've never said those words, never felt the urge.

Juan's Adam's apple bobs up and down. "I understand. I'm here if you need anything," he says.

I enter the room and click the door closed behind me. Gran's bedroom is as it always was, the bed neatly made with her ruffled blue bedspread, her pillows plump and wrinkle-free. On her bedside table is the heart-shaped brass jewelry box I gave her for Christmas many years ago. I lie down on her bed, curling into a ball and nestling my head into her pillow. "Gran," I say out loud. "I don't know what to do. I'm lost, and I'm all alone."

Getting lost is the first step to being found.

The tears come strong and fast, and only when Gran's pillow is steeped in my sorrow do I finally surrender to sleep. I'm startled awake by a muted knock on Gran's door. The knob turns and the door opens slowly. Juan stands in the shadows at the threshold.

"Molly, it's late," he whispers. "Are you sleeping in there tonight?"

"Yes," I reply.

"Okay," he says. "Molly, whatever I did to hurt you, I am so, so sorry. I love you more than anything in the world. I know you don't want to talk right now, but everything will look better in the morning. I promise."

With the lights out, I can barely make out his face in the hallway. I turn away from him and focus instead on the only light emanating from Gran's room—the heart-shaped brass jewelry box shining brightly in the dark.

Chapter 10

When I wake, it takes a moment to orient myself. Why am I in Gran's room? Then I remember . . .

I reach up behind me and open the curtains. The light falls across Gran's bed, bathing everything in a warm glow. It's true what Juan said last night and what Gran used to say—everything looks better in the morning light. Nothing has changed from yesterday to today, but somehow I feel a bit better.

I don't know why it comes to me, but suddenly I recall that old childhood game played with a daisy—pick a petal, *he loves me;* pick the next, *he loves me not.* It occurs to me that for every petal I've plucked lately, I've drawn but one conclusion, allowing for no other: *he loves me not.* In the light of day, I have to wonder: have I been going about this all wrong, plucking and plucking until the flower isn't even a flower anymore but a bare and spindly stem?

Accentuate the positive, eliminate the negative.

It gives me an idea. What if I search for evidence that he loves me instead of fixating on the proof that he does not?

I hear Juan stirring in the kitchen. He's humming "White Christmas" as he prepares our breakfast. I can smell the scent of coffee drifting through the crack under the door.

I get out of Gran's bed and head directly to the kitchen. I stand in the doorway underneath the sprig of mistletoe. Juan, bare-chested, his hair a rumpled mess, scrambles eggs for two on the stove. The bags under his eyes are the darkest they've ever been, and yet when he sees me, his eyes light up like our little misfit Christmas tree. He doesn't speak, but I know it's not the silent treatment. He's waiting for me to speak first.

"I'm sorry about last night," I say. "I know it's not right to go to bed angry, but I felt overwhelmed and didn't know what else to do."

"*Mi amor,*" he says. "It's okay."

"I have just one more question for you, if you don't mind me posing it," I say.

He turns off the stove and puts his spatula down. "Ask me anything." He faces me, his eyes serious, his chest exposed.

"Two days ago, you asked me a question, and I want to pose the same one to you. What do you want for Christmas more than anything else?"

He doesn't even deliberate. It takes him no time to answer. "You," he replies.

"But you're smart and handsome and hardworking. You

could have any other woman in the world. Are you sure that I'm enough?"

"*What?* You're more than enough. You've always been more than you ever give yourself credit for. You're everything."

I often have trouble reading the nuances of a face. And while most people are a mystery to me, Juan is an open book. Now, as I gaze at him, I see nothing in his face but love.

"Molly," he says, "whatever questions you still have for me, I'll answer them all. And just know, I have a question for you, too, a very important one. But you've guessed what I want to ask, haven't you?"

"Have I?" I reply.

His brow furrows and his head tilts to one side. "You don't know?"

"I'm afraid not," I say. "But go ahead. Ask your question."

"I will," he says. "But not now."

"If not now, when?" I ask.

"Very soon."

Chapter 11

The suspension of disbelief. Dictionary definition: to believe something is true even though it seems impossible.

That is the peace I have come to this morning, at least for the time being. I will spend the day looking for proof that Juan loves me instead of proof that he does not. Once the Christmas party is behind us, Juan and I will sit calmly and talk everything through. But now, we must focus on the big day ahead.

On our way to work, Juan is jumpier than I've ever seen him. He startles every time a bird flies by or a car honks its horn.

"If you're worried about the holiday staff party," I say, "you don't need to be. It's going to go fine."

"I'm hoping for the best," he replies. "Accentuate the positive, eliminate the negative, right?"

"Correct," I reply.

We arrive at the hotel, where my gran-dad is standing at his podium on the red-carpeted stairs. He ambles down the second he spots us.

"The beautiful couple has arrived," he says as he throws an arm around each of us, pulling us into his Father Christmas greatcoat.

"I've got to get to work right away," Juan says. "Mr. Preston, you catch up with Molly, okay? Have a good, long chat, you understand?" he says as he takes the stairs two by two and disappears through the revolving front doors.

"Don't ask me what that was all about," I say the moment Juan's gone. "He's been acting strange lately. And as for a good, long chat, I hardly have the time. Nor do you by the look of things."

Hordes of guests are leaving the hotel while new ones arrive in taxis and airport limousines.

"Oh, my dear girl," my gran-dad says. "None of that matters. Today is a very special day."

"Don't tell me you're in a tizzy over this staff Christmas party, too. Juan is beside himself."

Before I even know what's happening, my gran-dad wraps me in a hug so tight I fear I may burst at the seams. When he releases me, I see his eyes are wet. He pulls out his hankie to wipe tears away.

"What on earth has gotten into you?" I ask.

"I . . . I can't quite say," he replies.

"Well, there, there," I reply as I pat his arm. "No need for tears over a Christmas party."

He recovers and puts his hankie away. "I'll see you at noon?" he asks.

"You will," I reply as I head up the stairs and make my way through the gold revolving doors.

The hotel lobby looks even more resplendent today than it did yesterday. It's as though elves worked through the night to add more touches of Christmas cheer. Giant silver snowflakes hang from the ceiling on invisible strings, and the tree is lit and shining bright. The area around it is cordoned off for the party, and beneath it are stacks of beautifully wrapped gifts, delivered by Secret Santas in preparation for today's festivities.

The grand staircase has new decorations, too. Fresh garlands wind down the brass railings, and at the bottom, on the last stair, is a holiday décor piece I've never seen before—an enchanting evergreen archway that looks like the entrance to a magical Christmas land. Dangling from its center is a sprig of mistletoe held by a red velvet ribbon. As I take in the scene before me, I breathe deeply, the fragrances commingling in the air—pine needles and mulled cider, cinnamon and spice.

Mr. Snow is standing by the cordons, giving instructions to a valet. "Molly!" he calls out when he spots me.

I walk over as the valet trots away. "What do you think?" he asks, holding a hand up to the gloriously festive scene behind him.

"You've outdone yourself, Mr. Snow," I say. "The hotel has never looked better. But why go to such lengths this year?"

"Look your best for every guest—advice straight from your

handbook, Molly. It applies as much to our lobby as it does to our staff, don't you agree?"

A blush rises in my cheeks. "I heartily agree, Mr. Snow. But I must get going. Much to do today before noon. See you then with bells on?"

Mr. Snow jingles his corsage. "I wouldn't miss it for the world."

The rest of my morning is spent toiling upstairs with the other maids. We're working hard to clean as many rooms as possible before the commencement of our holiday party, when Housekeeping will be down to a skeleton staff, as will all departments in the hotel. Remarkably, even Cheryl is pulling her weight today, for the most part.

That being said, after a couple of hours laboring under my supervision, Cheryl does her usual disappearing act, carting laundry out of the room we're supposed to be cleaning together and never returning. By the time I've changed the sheets, vacuumed the floor into Zen garden lines, sanitized all glossy surfaces, and scrubbed until the washroom is spotlessly clean, there's still no sign of her. I wheel my trolley out of the room to look for her. It doesn't take long to spot her. She's just down the hall, leaning on Sunitha's trolley as Sunitha and Sunshine replenish it with supplies. I make my way over.

"I saw him with my own eyes, and so did she. Mr. Dishy was up to something fishy," she says with a hearty guffaw.

"Cheryl," I cut in, my voice a sharp blade. She jumps at the sound, knocking over a tower of toilet paper on the trolley, which Sunitha bends to collect before the rolls make their way farther down the hall.

"Cheryl, what were you just saying?" I ask. "Something about Juan Manuel?"

She stares at me, mouth opening and closing like that of a fish out of water.

"She was saying something so ridiculous it doesn't bear repeating," Sunshine offers as she dumps a handful of miniature shampoos into the tray on Sunitha's trolley.

"It's no secret," says Cheryl. "Molly saw him, too."

"I swear," says Sunshine, "if you open that piehole of yours one more time, I'll take one of these little shampoo bottles, pour the contents into your mouth, and scrub it clean myself."

"You shouldn't spread rumors," Sunitha adds. "It's wrong."

They both appear ready to hop over the trolley and scratch Cheryl's eyes out.

"Now, now," I say. "I realize Cheryl's affinity for spreading intracompany news often surpasses our internal memos, but in this case she's right. Juan Manuel *was* upstairs yesterday. In a guest's room."

"Maybe he was," says Sunshine, "but there must be a good reason why."

"Or Cheryl has the facts wrong," Sunitha adds. "As usual."

Sunshine checks her watch and sighs. "Molly, it's noon. It's time for the party. Can we let this go? Clean the slate? Wipe it away for another day?"

"There's nothing I'd rather do than that," I reply.

After parking the trolleys in the housekeeping quarters and refreshing ourselves in the change rooms, I lead the maids upstairs. Fortunately, the tension brewing among them earlier seems to have abated, at least for now. And as for whatever Juan was doing in that woman's room yesterday, I'm just not going to think about it right now. Maybe Sunitha's right—the facts are not what they seem.

When we arrive at the lobby, staff members are streaming in from various hotel departments. There's Mr. Preston, sans greatcoat but still wearing his Santa hat. He's chatting with the valets and bellhops, sipping on mulled cider, and chuckling as he listens to some story or other about long-departed guests. Beside the glittering Christmas tree are the receptionists, dressed in black and white, like neat little penguins. They've helped themselves to red-and-green iced cookies and cupcakes from silver trays on a long serving table—Juan's creations, no doubt—and now they take seats on the plush emerald settees. The kitchen staff are arriving, too. They duck under the cordon, heading straight for the beverage and sweets table, backslapping and complimenting each other on a job well done. Angela and her waitstaff join me and the maids by the magical evergreen archway at the bottom of the grand staircase. As I look about, I see almost everyone, including Mr. Snow. But one person is notably absent.

"Where's Juan Manuel?" I ask Angela as she takes her place by my side.

"How would I know?" she replies as she tucks an errant tress behind her ear.

Just then, Mr. Preston and Mr. Snow step forward.

"Attention, everyone!" Mr. Snow says as he taps a Regency Grand silver spoon against his Regency Grand porcelain teacup, which makes a pleasing tinkling sound. "Welcome to our staff holiday party. We've made it through another year of buzzing activity!" he says. "And all because of you, the worker bees."

"Omigawd, here he goes . . ." says Angela as she shades her eyes with one hand.

"We are a team, a family, a colony," Mr. Snow continues. "As devoted bees, you have cultivated and cared for our hotel hive all year long, and now, during this festive season, we reap the honey," he says as he points to the array of delectable sweets laid out on the serving table.

"So who's our Queen?" one of the bellhops calls out.

Titters and whispers, laughs and jeers, but I don't join in. Whatever remarks Mr. Snow has prepared, he's clearly forgotten them. He sniffs and adjusts his cravat.

"What our dear colleague and esteemed hotel manager is trying to say," says Mr. Preston, "is thank you to one and all for everything you do to make this workplace great. I, for one, am grateful."

"Here, here!" says Mr. Snow. "And since you're already by the tree and wearing the right hat, I nominate you, Mr. Preston, to be Santa's little helper. Will you pass out the Secret Santa gifts?"

"Ho, ho, ho!" says Mr. Preston. "Let's find out who's been naughty and nice."

As he passes out presents, I search the room for the one face I'm looking for, but Juan Manuel is still nowhere to be seen. Where could he be? How could he miss the party he worked so hard to throw?

There's no time to ask anyone these questions, for the staff have begun to open their gifts one by one. A sous-chef from Juan's team receives a "top chef" apron and joyously puts it on. A receptionist opens a white box full of Christmas cookies and gobbles one immediately. Mr. Preston is gifted a handmade scarf, which he wraps around his neck with glee. Angela opens her gift and is pleased to receive a bestselling true-crime book, used but in perfectly good condition. And when Cheryl opens her gift—a stack of old gossip mags—she's as thrilled as Cheryl ever gets.

"The crossword puzzles are filled in, but I guess that's okay," she says. "Thanks, whoever my Secret Santa is."

"You're welcome," Angela replies, then under her breath to me, "That's my good deed done for the year."

I poke her as a stern warning to hush.

"There are just two more gifts left under the tree," Mr. Preston announces as he hands Mr. Snow a small box I wrapped in brown paper earlier in the day.

"Go ahead, Mr. Snow. Open it," I say as the staff look on.

Mr. Snow removes the lid. His eyes grow wide and so unmistakably forlorn that while I know I'm not supposed to reveal my identity as the gift giver, I can't help myself.

"Don't you see?" I say. "It's a chain for your pocket watch so you never drop it again. I had it repurposed from a silver necklace my gran gave me years ago."

New creases appear on Mr. Snow's forehead, stacked over his eyebrows like pancakes on a platter.

"Aren't you going to try it on?" I prompt.

"I can't, Molly," Mr. Snow replies.

"Why not?" I ask.

"You'll have to open your gift to find out."

On cue, Mr. Preston reaches under the tree for the very last gift—the one meant for me. He places the shiny wrapped offering in my hands.

The box is small and dainty, no bigger than a tin of shoe polish. I remove the pretty paper and draw back the lid. Nestled inside, inlaid in a round silver medallion, is the most beautiful pendant made from one of my Head Maid name tags—MOLLY, HEAD MAID, it reads. I gasp out loud. "I love it! What a treasure!"

"But you can't wear it," says Mr. Snow. "Because you turned your necklace into a watch chain for me."

"No matter," I say. "I shall cherish this pendant regardless. And I'm pleased my necklace will be put to good use to protect your pocket watch from further mishaps."

"I'm afraid it won't, Molly," Mr. Snow explains. "That old watch of mine was always falling out of my pocket, so I upcycled the watch frame to have that pendant made for you."

"I can't believe my ears," says Mr. Preston. "It's like that old story by O. Henry—nothing goes right, but all is well in the end."

"Speaking of 'all's well in the end,' it's time," says Mr. Snow.

I'm about to announce to my maids that the party is over and we must get back to work, but before I can get a word out, my gran-dad puts a hand on my shoulder.

"There is one more gift, Molly."

"You mean for Juan Manuel?" I ask. "I'm afraid I don't know where he is."

"I mean for you."

Gran-dad turns and looks up, way up, at the shining star rising above the terrace on the very tippy top of the Christmas tree. But then something, or rather, someone, moves behind the tree. It's Juan. He steps out from the boughs and looks down at me from the starlit terrace. He's dressed in crisp chef whites but with a black bow tie around his neck. In his hands he holds a bouquet of red roses.

"Juan?" I exclaim as I look up at him. "What in heavens are you doing up there hiding behind the Christmas tree?"

Suddenly, all of my misgivings flood back—the comings and goings, the strange behaviors, the explanations that make no sense. I can't make heads or tails of any of it. And now, it's happening here, in public, before the entire hotel staff.

Waiters and receptionists titter and laugh. Bellhops and valets chortle out loud. It's déjà vu, like being haunted by the ghost of a Christmas past. Yet again, I've said something foolish, and I have no idea what it is.

"They're laughing at me, all of them," I whisper to Angela as I take in their jeering faces.

"They're laughing with you, not at you," she says. "I promise."

Just then, Juan descends the stairs, step by step, slowly, stopping on the final tread underneath the evergreen archway.

The laughing stops, and silence descends. Everyone gathered becomes so still that not a corsage jingles or a spoon tinkles. Somehow this hush is more discomfiting than any noise I've ever heard.

"Molly," Juan says, as he turns his dark-eyed gaze my way. "Will you join me?" He points to the archway above his head and the mistletoe dangling there.

I look at my gran-dad, searching his face for some clue as to what on earth is going on.

"It's all right, Molly. Come." He offers me an arm, and feeling quite unsteady, I take it, allowing him to lead me up the step to stand beside Juan under the archway.

"Molly," Juan says. "This morning I told you I have a question for you, and now, I'm going to ask it."

"You're going to ask it here?"

The crowd laughs again, and I feel the room tilt underneath my feet. I grab a garland-wrapped balustrade to keep myself steady and upright.

"Molly Gray, Head Maid and love of my life," Juan says, "will you marry me?"

Before I can even process the words, Juan reaches for a silver clamshell box tied on a gold ribbon around the bouquet of roses. He opens the box. Though I've seen it before, what's inside is confusing—a Claddagh ring, the one my gran-dad showed me yesterday, the one that was going to be given to some lucky young lady.

My chest is tight. My breath stops short, and suddenly, I'm seeing stars. I don't know if the lights twinkling in my peripheral vision are the tree's or my own. An arm grips me to keep me upright.

"Molly, please don't faint," says Juan.

His eyes are liquid chocolates. The moment they meet mine, my breath returns, and the room rights itself. Juan stands there, awaiting my reply.

"This question," I say. "You can't be serious. Why would you want to marry me?"

"Because *I do*!" he exclaims. "Except those two words are the ones I'd hoped *you'd* say, not me." He pauses, holding the bouquet and ring box in one hand while he wipes his brow with the other. "It wasn't supposed to go like this." He takes a deep breath and looks at me again. "Molly, I know you've had your doubts about me, especially lately, but they're unfounded. Nothing is as it seems."

His hands are shaking. The roses tremble.

"Red roses," I say. "Didn't I see these yesterday?"

"Yes," he says emphatically. "I brought them to Angela to hide in the storeroom of the Social, but then you caught me in flagrante, so I beelined out the back door."

I look at Angela.

"He sure did," she confirms. "A streak of red and white, like a candy cane on the run."

"And then, to make matters worse," Juan says, "Cheryl caught me upstairs going into that woman's room."

"Very fishy, Señor Dishy," Cheryl says with a waggle of her finger.

"Not fishy at all," says Mr. Snow. "I gave Juan my express permission to enter that guest's room. He's been baking extra Christmas cookies in the kitchen downstairs, earning a bit of extra money by offering them on consignment to hotel guests. Our guests love his baking, and it's bringing the hotel great publicity, too."

"Extra dough for extra dough," says Angela. "Get it, Molly?"

"A pun," I reply. "Understood. But why do you need extra dough?" I ask Juan.

"To buy you an engagement ring, a new one. I've been working as Mr. Rosso's superintendent for the last three months. That's why I'm racing around all the time when we're at home, fixing things and trying to hide what I'm up to. I made Mr. Rosso promise not to tell you. I wanted it to be a surprise."

Your affairs are none of my business. Mr. Rosso's words ring in my ears, another thing I've gotten wrong.

"I had the ring all picked out. But I didn't know your ring size, which is why my mom sent the *atrapanovios*."

"The stain on my finger."

"A measurement," says Juan. "Then I dragged you to that jewelry store to see how you felt about diamonds. I wanted to buy you a fancy new ring from that place. But when you said the bracelet on the poster was too expensive, I started to think maybe I messed up—that an expensive, new engagement ring wasn't what you'd want at all. Recycle and reuse. Waste not, want not. That's what you always say."

"And that's when Mr. Preston came up with an idea," Angela adds.

My gran-dad steps forward. "Molly, that Claddagh ring was your gran's," he explains. "I once put it on her finger, but it wasn't meant to be. I know for certain she cherished that ring and hoped with all her might that, though she never wore it on her ring finger, one day you'd wear it on yours."

I look down at the ring nestled in satin and shining like a star in the clamshell box. Oh, how I've gotten everything wrong—Juan's exhaustion, his mysterious disappearances, the women who meant nothing at all. I've done it again. I've misread all the clues.

"Juan," I say. "I'm so sorry. I assumed the worst of you instead of the best. I made an A-S-S, not out of U but out of ME. I see it now, all that you were trying to do—for us, for me." I look at him and see his eyes are glassy and he's on the verge of tears. He's been with me all along, right by my side, though I doubted him. He's put everything into this moment, and I long to make it right. "Will you please repeat your question one more time?" I ask.

Juan nods and his Adam's apple bobs. "Molly Gray," he says, "Head Maid and love of my life, will you marry me?"

There is only one answer. It was there all along, and now I see it, plain as day.

"Yes," I say. "I would be honored to be your wife."

Juan removes the ring from its box and gives the roses to Angela to hold. He slips the ring on my finger, a perfect fit—a heart held in hands that remind me of my gran's.

I have never been proposed to before. I don't know what to do next, so I curtsy. Everyone laughs.

"Molly, I know rules are important," Juan says, "and far be it from me to break one, but do you think that maybe just this once we could break our rule?" As he says this, he looks up at the archway above our heads and the mistletoe hanging there.

I look out at the staff, the maids gathered on one side, the cooks on the other, the bellhops and valets, the receptionists and waiters. Mr. Snow stands in front of them all, and Mr. Preston, the doorman (a.k.a. my gran-dad), has taken a place by his side. All of them, even Cheryl, have tears in their eyes.

I turn back to Juan Manuel. "What I think," I say, "is that you should kiss me."

Under the mistletoe, Juan's lips meet mine. They are lush and warm, and as I close my eyes, all my troubles, all my strife melts away. It's as if we're in a snow globe, a tiny perfect world where only the two of us exist.

Juan pulls away and his eyes meet mine.

Suddenly, I understand what I failed to comprehend before. Just like that, the mystery is solved. "A bride and groom!"

I exclaim. "The two figures! That's what you saw in the snow globe."

"Yes," Juan replies. "I saw our Christmas future. And I'm so glad you see it now, too."

When I was a child, my gran loved to entertain me with parables and fairy tales. She always put her own spin on them, embedding a moral or a warning of some kind.

Once, she told me the story of a maid who'd been wrongly accused of stealing a piece of silverware only for it to be discovered too late that a rat was the real culprit. She also told a tale about a poor young couple who were very much in love and wanted to exchange gifts at Christmas. The wife cut her hair to buy her husband a chain for his watch, and he sold his watch to buy her combs for her hair, rendering both gifts useless in the end, but it didn't matter. As Gran always knew, love is the only gift that lasts.

It is Christmas morning. Juan Manuel is humming carols in the kitchen and preparing a sumptuous brunch with more food than we'll ever be able to eat in one day. My gran-dad and Charlotte will arrive soon, wearing silly Christmas sweaters, laden with gifts and good cheer. We will eat and laugh and sing—all of us together, our special found family.

But before they arrive, I've slipped away for a quiet moment to myself. It's strange for me to come here twice in one week, to the room that used to be Gran's. I'm seated on her bed, holding a heart-shaped jewelry box in my hands. I look at the ring on my finger. It's a near-perfect match—my hands hold her heart, and her hands hold mine.

I open the box, and I swear on my life, I hear her voice, merry and bright, singing the last line of her favorite carol:

Have yourself a merry little Christmas now.

Acknowledgments

Being a writer feels like living in a snow globe—it's an insular, little world full of fantasy and wonder, but just one tremor can set off a storm. To all the people listed below, a thousand thanks for helping me through all kinds of weather:

My brilliant support team at the Madeleine Milburn Literary Agency, especially Madeleine Milburn, Rachel Yeoh, Valentina Paulmichl, Hannah Kettles, Giles Milburn, Saskia Arthur, Megan Capper, and Hannah Ladds.

My U.S. team at Ballantine, Penguin Random House: Hilary Teeman, Kara Welsh, Kim Hovey, Taylor Noel, Megan Whalen, Michelle Jasmine, Hope Hathcock, Diane McKiernan, Elena Giavaldi, Virginia Norey, Pamela Alders, Cindy Berman, Angela McNally, Sandra Sjursen, and Elsa Richardson-Bach.

My Canadian team at Penguin Canada: Nicole Winstanley (greatly missed!), Dan French (also greatly missed!), Kristin

Cochrane, Bonnie Maitland, Adria Iwasutiak, Beth Cockeram, Beth Lockley, Meredith Pal, Sabrina Papas, and Jasmin Shin.

My UK team at HarperFiction: Charlotte Brabbin, Emilie Chambeyron, Maddy Marshall, Holly Martin, Frankie Gray, Lynne Drew, Sarah Shea, Ellie Game, and Bethan Moore.

A very important early reader: Arlyn Miller-Lachmann.

My film and TV team: Josie Freedman, Josh McLaughlin, and Chris Goldberg.

My long-suffering friends: Sarah Fulton, Aileen Umali and Eric Rist, Martin Ortuzar and Ingrid Nasager, Roberto Verdecchia, Adria Iwasutiak, Janie Yoon, Sarah St. Pierre, Felicia Quon, Sarah Gibson, Jessica Scott, Ellen Keith, Matthew Lawson, and Zoe Maslow.

Last, but not least, my family, always: Tony Hanyk and Theo, Dan and Patty, Devin and Joane, Freddie and Pat, and Jackie and Paul.

About the Author

Nita Prose is the #1 *New York Times* bestselling author of *The Mystery Guest* and *The Maid,* which has sold more than two million copies worldwide. A *Good Morning America* Book Club pick, *The Maid* won the Ned Kelly Award for International Crime Fiction, the Fingerprint Award for Debut Book of the Year, the Anthony Award for Best First Novel, and the Barry Award for Best First Mystery. *The Maid* was also an Edgar Award finalist for Best Novel. Visit Nita at nitaprose.com.

X and Instagram: @NitaProse

About the Type

This book was set in Albertina, a typeface created by Dutch calligrapher and designer Chris Brand (1921–98). Brand's original drawings, based on calligraphic principles, were modified considerably to conform to the technological limitations of typesetting in the early 1960s. The development of digital technology later allowed Frank E. Blokland (b. 1959) of the Dutch Type Library to restore the typeface to its creator's original intentions.

From #1 *New York Times* bestselling author

NITA PROSE

"Excellent and totally entertaining . . .
the most interesting (and endearing)
main character in a long time."

—STEPHEN KING

Order now

NitaProse.com **@NitaProse**